Praise for

Chloe

"In this entertaining riff on *Rebecca* from bestseller Briscoe (*You Never Know*), a young chef embarks on a whirlwind romance with a billionaire. . . . Briscoe folds some perceptive class critiques into her intoxicating blend of romance and suspense. This offers plenty of gothic pleasures."

—*Publishers Weekly*

"*Chloe* is a fresh and thrilling take on Daphne du Maurier's *Rebecca*. If you loved the original, you will love this version, too."

—Karin Slaughter, *New York Times* bestselling author of *Pretty Girls*

Also by Connie Briscoe

Chloe

A Novel of
Secrets and Lies

Connie
Briscoe

AMISTAD

An Imprint of HarperCollins*Publishers*

HarperCollins books may be purchased for educational, business, or sales promotional use. For information, please email the Special Markets Department at SPsales@harpercollins.com.

harpercollins.com

FIRST AMISTAD PAPERBACK PUBLISHED IN 2026

Designed by Kyle O'Brien
Title page art © asadulhoque/Shutterstock

Library of Congress Cataloging-in-Publication Data
is available upon request.

ISBN 978-0-06-333857-9

Printed in the United States of America

26 27 28 29 30 LBC 5 4 3 2 1

This one is for my family and friends—Karen Singleton,
Diane Singleton, Nate Whitaker, Shirley Whitaker,
Patty DeJarnett, and many more—who make
Martha's Vineyard such a joyful, fun,
and relaxing place to visit.

Sometime in the Future

There it was again. The nightmare. Creeping up, invading.

She was running, faster, faster. Stumbling across the dusty, damp grounds of Riverwild. Over a soggy lawn, through the weed-strangled garden, to the top of a slick hillside.

She stopped, breathless, her chest heaving; gazed up at the night sky; and tried to quiet her wildly thumping heart. Then she peered down below. The waters of the mighty Potomac River spread out before her, raging to and fro. She glanced back at the mansion, looming tall and menacingly, its dark and deadly secrets now completely exposed.

Standing there on the hill all alone, she felt a wailing cry bubble up in her throat. She was more confused than ever. She had anticipated a life filled with love, joy, tenderness. Not secrets and lies. Not bullets and blood.

That wife of yours is dangerous . . . Caught her snooping . . . How much does she know?

Nothing. Not a single thing.

That was then.

Now she knew everything.

And she had never been more frightened.

Part 1

1

The day had started out decent enough, with bright clouds floating above.

Then thunder clapped. The sky went dark.

Not the kind of weather you hoped for when boarding the ferry to Martha's Vineyard, Angel thought, her flip-flops squeaking across the damp passenger ramp at the Steamship Authority terminal. Wheeling her luggage along, she dashed inside and made her way to a seat just as heavy rain fell.

This was her third year visiting Martha's Vineyard while working as a private chef but the first time she'd traveled in such miserable conditions. Unless one counted the last of many summers she'd visited with her parents as an enthusiastic young girl who loved to sketch and dreamed of someday becoming an artist. That had been twenty years ago, when the family ended up stuck on the island for three frightful days as an unusually early hurricane pummeled the land and all transportation to and from it was halted. Now she traveled by plane and bus, but back then she and her parents always made the nearly five-hundred-mile trek by car from Washington, DC, to Woods Hole, Massachusetts, then hopped on the ferry. That had been the summer ritual for their little family of three right up until the year of the hurricane. The same year her dad lost his restaurant business and the family lost their precious Victorian-style house in Northwest DC, along with their Volvo station wagon. And her mother eventually walked out and left their tidy little family.

She had been barely twelve years old the summer her world toppled upside down. Neither of her parents would talk to her in much detail about what had happened between them, or why. Angel had often imagined that if her mother had run off and left her only child, it must have been to go someplace very special. Maybe some magical destination in a faraway land. Angel would eventually pick up bits of the ugly truth here and there from soft whisperings among cousins and aunts at family gatherings. Would see the quiet look of desperation on her father's face whenever she stole a glance as he whipped up a meal for the two of them in their tiny, sparsely furnished two-bedroom apartment. Still, she clung furiously to the belief that nothing could have enticed her mom away from them short of a place resembling paradise.

That childhood fantasy was shattered when her mom remarried about a year after taking off and sent for her daughter. That was when the annual summer visits to Richmond, Virginia, began, and her dreams of becoming an artist came to an abrupt halt. By then she was thirteen and eons wiser about the temptations and jealousies that could quickly sour a relationship.

Her current boyfriend, Gene, seemed to be on a mission to prove this very point. She and a few co-workers had dropped into the neighborhood club late one summer night after work and one of them pointed out that the sexy drummer onstage was eyeing her. She'd turned and given him a little smile, and one thing led quickly to another. He had the kind of seductive look that sent chills up and down a girl's spine. Within days she and Gene were an item, going everywhere together—concerts, parks, his place or hers.

After a couple of happy, carefree months, it slowly dawned on Angel that other women were probably having similar experiences with Gene. That she wasn't all that special. She'd been down this route a time or two before and knew what it looked and felt like when a man's interests had drifted elsewhere. He didn't call or text as often, didn't compliment her as frequently. Didn't even look at her in the same way. He would become furtive, evasive.

By the time she left for her stay on the island in early August, she and Gene had agreed to take a temporary break. When she got back to DC at the end of the month, they were going to have a long talk. She was still into Gene and really wanted to work things out. Not to mention that she was thirty-three years old and hated the thought of facing yet another failed relationship.

She settled into a seat near the window on the ferry, nursing a cup of black coffee. Odd that all these negative memories came flooding back to her at this moment. It must be the sight of rain and rough seas relentlessly pounding the boat as they ripped and rocked across the choppy sound. At one point she had to grab the paper coffee cup to keep it from sliding off the table. She glanced around, anxiously wondering if she should be concerned for her safety while on these choppy seas. Others on the boat, most probably year-round residents or decades-long summer vacationers, seemed completely unfazed. Still, she couldn't help feeling rattled. She was not used to being heaved and hurled about in the middle of the Atlantic. Maybe she should have stayed at home. Had that heart-to-heart talk with Gene sooner rather than later. At least it was safe there. She had taken up sketching again last summer while visiting the island, having been inspired by the sheer beauty of the landscape just as she had been as a girl. She decided to try drawing the blurry shore of Cape Cod as it slowly disappeared beyond the thick raindrops glistening on the window. Hopefully that would calm her nerves.

At last the sun peeked out from the clouds just as the boat docked at the Oak Bluffs terminal forty-five minutes later. The moment Angel reached the end of the ramp and hit the sidewalk, her mood brightened. The old memories fell away. The island was a far cry from her life in the city. Everything felt different here—the pace slower, the sky brighter, the ocean breeze cooler, the people friendlier. The place had a magnetic pull on all who landed on its sandy shores, encouraging them to leave their troubles behind—and goodness knew she had her share—to allow the wholesome aura to envelope and soothe their weary souls— old and young, Black and white, businessman and beachgoer, rich and poor alike. And they heeded the call. Their differences— often crushingly disruptive at home—were willingly tossed aside into the depths of the sea. At least on the surface.

She smiled at the touch of the salty ocean breeze gracing her brown cheeks and skipping through her curly shoulder-length hair as she tugged her luggage along Seaview Avenue. The roar of the mighty waves ripping along the sandy beach beside her was like music to her ears. She had about a six-block-long walk to the Harrison house and had long since learned to pack lightly, even though it was a monthlong trip—a few sundresses, shorts and capris, and short-sleeve cotton tops and tees, all folded neatly and stuffed into a single suitcase and one tote.

She squinted ahead until she could make out the grand covered porch wrapped around the Victorian house owned by the Harrisons. The sprawling, weathered shingle-style home sat among a row of large houses overlooking Nantucket Sound. Many of the Black families who had summerhouses in this section of Oak Bluffs had owned them for more than a century, having first purchased in the early 1900s, when hotels in the area had turned them away. Now they passed their cherished houses along from one generation to the next.

The Harrisons were an exception as relative newcomers to the area, having purchased their house a mere decade earlier. They summered on the island every year, from June to August. Jillian Harrison usually spent the entire three months there, whereas her husband Irvin and their twenty-nine-year-old daughter, Norma, traveled back home to Washington, DC, during the week to work. They joined Jillian for the month of August, when the family threw a lavish garden party on the expansive lawn attended by about one hundred guests.

Jillian and Irvin had a strange relationship, at least in Angel's opinion, she thought as she wheeled her luggage through the door of the white gate that surrounded the property. They were in their fifties and had been married for a few decades. The honeymoon phase was long since over, and the distance between them seemed vast. Angel could never once remember seeing the two touch each other. Or even smile at each other. He did his thing— mainly tennis and golf; and Jillian did hers—lunch and gallery events with friends. Their bespectacled daughter, Norma, seemed to have few friends on the island and could usually be found down on the nearby Inkwell Beach in the early-morning hours before the crowds descended or somewhere on the grounds of the house reading a book. The family came together now and then at social gatherings for what seemed to Angel to be purely for the sake of appearances.

Angel knew that many of the Black colleges had a huge presence on the island. As did Black students who had attended the Ivy Leagues and other prestigious schools. Jillian had attended a small college in Georgia. Her husband had attended Cornell University, and many of the Black alumni spent summers there. But Irvin had little interest in their social events. So Jillian had

had to work tirelessly to make acquaintances over the years, with help here and there from her better-connected sorority sisters. She wanted everything at her annual gathering of doctors and lawyers and businessmen and businesswomen to be absolutely flawless. She had convinced Pierre, the chef at Georgia's, one of her favorite restaurants in DC, to allow Angel, a sous-chef there, to take the month of August off to come and work as a private chef for the Harrison family. A little gift of several thousand dollars donated each year to Pierre's favorite restaurant charity had helped secure the favor.

Angel had no real complaints. Although she found some people on the island pretentious and uppity, including Jillian's friends, she readily welcomed the break from the hot, humid, and tourist-filled summers in DC. And the brief chance to enjoy living life as the other half did. With its soaring ceilings, spacious rooms, and multiple screened porches, the house was a far cry from the small cottages and hotel rooms she vaguely recalled staying in with her parents when they'd visited. As lovely as their lodgings had been, they couldn't compare to this, one of the premiere houses in Oak Bluffs. The massive chef's kitchen was a dream to work in.

As Angel let herself into the foyer with her key, her mind quickly turned to the busy days she had ahead as they prepared for Friday's event, only a couple of days away. It was already nearly two o'clock, and she had to get together with Jillian to plan the menu, shop for food, and begin early preparations. On the big day she would help Jillian supervise the temporary staff that would set up tables, decorations, and food on the lawn. Angel only hoped neither Irvin nor Norma had taken the family Benz SUV. She hadn't seen it parked in the driveway or along the street and would need it for shopping.

She was about to climb the wide staircase just off the center hallway to go to her room and freshen up—Jillian was not a fan of the cutoff jeans and flip-flops she was wearing, or any kind of jeans for that matter—when she heard her boss's voice calling from the rear of the house.

"Angel, is that you?"

Angel immediately picked up the hint of annoyance in Jillian's voice and braced herself. Jillian paused as she emerged from the kitchen area, the skirt of her flowered dress blowing breezily with each step. Her plump figure, youthful and fair-complexioned face—courtesy of expensive spa treatments galore—and boundless energy level helped Jillian appear ten years younger than her fifty-two years. "Goodness. Thank God you're back, finally," she said upon laying eyes on Angel. Her face wore a half smile, half frown. "I was expecting you hours ago. We have so much to do."

Angel cleared her throat. "Yes, Mrs. Harrison. My flight was late leaving DC and . . ." Not entirely true, a tiny voice in Angel's head whispered as the words she had rehearsed on the plane tumbled forth. The embarrassing truth was that Gene had been late picking her up to take her to the airport and she'd missed her flight. She hated lying but didn't want to admit that her boyfriend was getting so unreliable. Besides, she knew Jillian would never understand, given that she considered this the most important event of the year for her. As pushy as Jillian could be, Angel loved spending summers on the island and would hate to lose this job.

"I'm really sorry, Mrs. Harrison," Angel said. "I just need a minute to freshen up and . . ."

"Well, go on then," Jillian said abruptly, giving a firm look of disapproval to Angel's attire and a wave of her perfectly manicured hand. "And be quick about it. We must finish planning this menu so you can get going with the shopping. Irvin is out playing tennis but promised me he would be back by three so you can take the car and . . ."

Angel didn't hear the rest; she dashed up the stairs as quickly as she could manage with her luggage. In the hall bathroom she splashed water on her face and washed up. Then she changed into an off-white linen dress and skipped quickly down the stairs.

* * *

She and Jillian were sitting at the long, rustic walnut kitchen table finalizing a menu consisting of several fruit-and-cheese boards, salmon sliders, and berry and seafood salads with macarons for dessert when Irvin returned. She heard him drop the keys on the table near the front door and bound up the stairs without uttering so much as a syllable to anyone. Jillian's phone rang, and Angel picked up the menu and stood, preparing to leave. She had her work cut out for her and wanted to get going.

Jillian had other ideas. "Hold on just a minute," she said, lifting a finger to silence Angel as she continued speaking into the phone. Angel waited patiently until she hung up. "I need you to do something else for me first."

"If you mean dinner, I can start on that as soon as I get back. The market closes at five and . . ."

"There's been a change of plans," Jillian said abruptly. "You'll have time to shop tomorrow morning if you go early. And we won't be eating in tonight. We're having dinner at Nancy's. I just heard that none other than Everett Bruce will be there."

Jillian smiled so broadly that Angel had the feeling she should know who this Everett Bruce was. But she hadn't a clue. She frowned with puzzlement.

"From the look on your face," Jillian said, "I take it that you have no idea who he is."

Angel shook her head. "Should I?"

Jillian scoffed, strode to a bookcase, and began to rifle through a shelf full of books and glossy magazines. "Now where did I put my copy of *Executive Magazine*?" she said, rifling through copies of *Forbes* and *Fortune*. "He was on the cover of the last issue. In fact, he's been on the cover a few times. I'm shocked you've never heard of him. He's a billionaire, founder and CEO of a private equity firm."

Angel shrugged. As a private chef, she considered herself an entrepreneur and definitely took an interest in business. She had even read *Executive Magazine* a few times and knew that despite being a newcomer, it was quickly climbing the ranks in readership. But what Jillian was talking about seemed to be a whole different level of "business," far removed from anything remotely connected to her. "Can't say that I have."

Jillian scoffed again at the expression on Angel's face. "Good grief. There are only about fifteen Black billionaires in the entire world according to *Forbes*, you know. And half of them are in Africa. Everett Bruce is American born and bred, from a small town in Virginia. He owns a fabulous estate on the river in Potomac, Maryland, called Riverwild. It was once owned by Arabian royalty."

Jillian whispered that last bit like it was a highly guarded state secret. Angel nodded, now mildly impressed but still confused as to what all this had to do with her.

"He's donated millions to support Blacks in higher education and . . ." Jillian paused, slipped the magazine back onto the shelf. "I can't seem to find the piece about him. Although I shouldn't be surprised you have no interest in these things."

Angel winced at her boss's words. Jillian was always comparing Angel's community college associate of arts degree unfavorably to Norma's bachelors from Smith College, or any four-year college. Angel wanted to remind Jillian that her little two-year degree in culinary arts was good enough for her to cook at the posh events she threw every summer and deserved more respect. Still, she kept her thoughts to herself. These were the moments she had to remind herself how much she loved getting paid to come to this serene and beautiful island every summer.

"Anyway, I recently got word through a very credible source that Everett is vacationing here the entire month," Jillian said. "Can you believe it? He's staying over in Edgartown, not far from the Obamas. Everyone is talking about it."

Angel twisted her mouth in a half smile, half frown as she struggled to keep her growing annoyance with Jillian off her face. No, not everyone, she thought. *She* was not talking about it. Nor was Gene or anyone else she knew for that matter. And she still had no idea why Jillian was making such a big fuss and changing their well-thought-out plans. She fidgeted with her fingers, waited for Jillian to go on.

"He's a billionaire," Jillian repeated. "And he did not make his fortune in sports or entertainment. That's remarkable. We need more like him representing us, you know."

Angel shifted from one foot to the other. Yes, she'd heard that the first time, and yes, she knew just how unusual an accomplishment it was. She didn't need Jillian lecturing her.

"His wife passed away recently," Jillian continued. "Very suddenly."

Now *that* got Angel's attention. She had a vague memory of reading about the death of a very prominent woman in Maryland in the *Washington Post* online about a year ago. Although she could recall few details. "Really? Sorry to hear that."

"Yes, such a tragedy. But enough about that. I've met him once or twice at social events—her, too, before she passed—and I want to try and catch him to invite him to my gathering on Friday, introduce him to Norma. He's in his forties so quite a bit older but very fit for a man his age. At Nancy's, they don't do reservations. It's first come, first served."

Angel was finally beginning to sense where all this was leading. Jillian wanted her to run up to the restaurant and wait in line for the family. She did not like this idea at all; she was a chef, not a line stander. Besides, Norma didn't seem like the type who would enjoy having her mother fix her up. She was quiet and shy and preferred to keep to herself, at least when she was here on the island. She mostly read and sometimes played tennis with her father. Based on the few conversations Angel'd had with Norma, it seemed her main life was back at home in Northern Virginia where she had a condo and a small, tight circle of friends. She came to the island to relax and spend quality time with her folks. Angel frowned with intent, hoping Jillian would catch the look of disapproval and think twice about what she was about to ask.

No such luck.

"Since Irvin is upstairs probably showering and Norma is still down at the beach, we can't leave for a bit. I was hoping you would be a sweetheart and run over to Nancy's to put our names on the list while we get ready and . . ."

"You want me to stay and wait until you all get there," Angel finished for her. Obviously, the intentional look had had zero impact on Jillian.

"Yes," Jillian said, smiling delightedly. "Exactly."

Angel took a deep breath. The popular restaurant was on the water and had large windows overlooking Oak Bluffs Harbor. A forty-five-minute or longer wait for a table was not uncommon, especially during the popular month of August, when the population of the island swelled from about seventeen thousand year-round residents to two hundred thousand, including visitors during the peak of the summer season. Angel shifted from one foot to the other. "I'm not sure I . . ."

Before she could continue to protest, Jillian grabbed Angel's purse from the kitchen table and shoved it into her arms. "The sooner you get going, the sooner you can get us a table. We won't be long."

Angel was speechless. She wanted to tell Jillian *absolutely not*. She had no intention of waiting around for a table when she was not even invited to join them for the meal. Not that she had expected an invitation, but still, this was insulting.

"Think of it this way," Jillian said, smiling sweetly, "at least you won't have to prepare dinner tonight. You can relax and help yourself to anything in the fridge. Maybe do some sketching from one of the screened porches or down at the beach. It's so pretty there in the evening."

Angel gripped her handbag. The idea of a quiet evening sketching, one of her favorite things to do besides cooking, and having the house all to herself didn't seem half bad. "Okay, I'll go." But just this once, she thought as she walked toward the front door.

"And text me if you see him there," Jillian called after her. "He's tall, with a smooth, dark complexion and salt-and-pepper hair. Everyone will probably be staring in his direction. I'm going to get Norma now. We'll be right behind you."

Angel turned and rolled her eyes skyward. She grabbed a big rubber band from a drawer and tied her thick hair into a ponytail to keep it off her neck as she exited. It was hot and steamy, and she had quite a walk ahead of her. How silly, she thought as her sandaled feet hit the pavement. A thousand men on this island could fit Jillian's description. The restaurant was about a half mile away. Normally, it was a walk she would enjoy. But she was exhausted from the journey that afternoon. First by Uber to the airport, then the flight to Boston, followed by a long ride on the Peter Pan Bus, and finally the ferry to the island. And this was the hottest time of the day. She should be in an air-conditioned car driving to an air-conditioned market to shop for food, something that always made her feel good. Cooking was her happy place. Running up to a restaurant for an inconsiderate employer and chasing after a man she knew practically nothing about, nor cared to, was not how she'd envisioned spending her first evening back on the island.

She entered the restaurant, climbed the stairs to the main area, and threaded her way through the diners near the entrance lined up for a table. She was not surprised at all when told it would take fifty minutes to an hour to be seated. Still, the thought of such a long wait was exasperating. She only hoped the Harrisons would hurry up and arrive so she could get out of there. The heavy but heavenly scent of seafood filling the room was almost unbearable, as it reminded her that she hadn't eaten for hours and was nearly starving.

A waiter passed by bearing a tray piled high with scallops, shrimp, and vegetables. It looked mouthwatering. She would love to try creating her own version in a tomatoey soup. She spotted an empty area near the entrance and made her way toward it as she rummaged through her shoulder bag in search of the small writing pad she used to jot down her thoughts for the cookbook she had been working on now for several months. Whenever she thought of a new recipe idea to try, she wrote it down, along with possible ingredients.

She was jerked out of her reverie when she stumbled awkwardly over a sandal-clad foot sticking out in front of her. She managed to catch herself just in time, but the writing pad popped straight up and out of her hands, tumbling to the floor. Before she could retrieve it, a man wearing khakis and a Panama fedora pulled low over his forehead scooped it up.

"Soups and salads. Recipes," he said, reading her scribbling on the front cover. He smiled as he held it out to her; she smiled thinly in return, feeling clumsy and embarrassed, and quickly looked away. No one in the entire world knew she was working on a recipe book, and she preferred to keep it that way.

"Thank you," she said, and walked off to squeeze into a small space along the wall. It was so tight she had to turn sideways to be able to write on her pad.

Forty minutes later, the Harrison family showed up.

"Any sightings?" Jillian asked as soon as Angel approached them, raising her voice to a high whisper to be heard above the noisy crowd.

Angel shook her head wearily as the Harrisons were called. Thank goodness, Angel thought as the hostess approached them. She had just reached the stairs to the exit when she heard Jillian exclaim, "Oh, I see him. He's here." Angel glanced back to see Jillian grab a perplexed-looking Norma's hand and dash off in front of Irvin and the hostess, presumably making a beeline to the wonderful Mr. Bruce. Angel almost felt sorry for the man, but she could not even pretend to be any more interested than that. This was finally her chance to escape. She darted down the stairs and out the door.

2

On the big day, dreary clouds floated above as Angel made her quick run to Morning Glory to pick up a few last-minute items. The weather was not looking promising for a garden party. But there wasn't a darn thing she or anyone else could do about that, she thought as she picked over the fresh baked goods at the farm-stand, except pray the weather forecast would prove accurate and that brighter skies indeed lay ahead. For her sake as well as Jillian's. Nothing dampened the summer Harrison household more quickly and dramatically than one of her boss's foul, unforgiving moods. Long, bitter tirades directed at the family and staff were not unheard of. Angel had been on the receiving end once or twice herself.

As she lugged multiple grocery bags stuffed with fresh fruits and vegetables up the side stairs to the kitchen door, Angel spotted Jillian on the lawn, still in her frilly bathrobe and dainty slippers, her long hair wrapped in a colorful scarf. She and Maria, the event planner, were supervising a half dozen workers setting up tables and festive decorations on the expansive lawn for what Angel could see was going to be yet another lavish sit-down luncheon. She dropped her bags on the kitchen countertop, then promptly set out several gleaming pots and pans on the six-burner gas range. Jillian had hired a couple of freelance chefs, who should arrive shortly, and the guests were expected a couple of hours after that. She needed to have everything prepped and ready to go for them.

"Oh, there you are," Jillian said as the screen door shut behind her. "I hope you were able to get everything we need."

Angel nodded. "Take a look at that gorgeous fresh corn," she said as she fired up the oven. "Looks perfect for my chilled corn soup and lobster salad."

"Sounds yummy," Jillian said. "Now all I need is for this horrid weather to cooperate."

"I think it'll be fine. You know how things can change on a dime here this time of year."

"Let's hope you're right, Angel. For once I . . ." Jillian paused as her gaze shifted to something behind Angel. "You're not wearing *that.*"

Angel turned to see Norma round the corner at the back staircase that led directly from the second floor to the kitchen. She had on dark gray knee-length shorts, a crisp white cotton shirt, and white Keds. As usual, her freckled face had not a trace of makeup; her light brown hair fell limply over her cheeks, looking barely combed. Angel smiled. Whereas Jillian was all about fluff and frills, Norma's style was plain and simple, even austere. Mother and daughter were polar opposites.

Norma looked down at her outfit. "It's a backyard picnic," she said with sarcasm. "What's wrong with this?"

"Lawn party, sweetie," Jillian said with mild annoyance. "It's a lawn party. You know better. You need to choose something brighter. And cuter. Don't forget how stylish our guests will be."

"Mom, this will be fine. I'm not a child. I know . . ."

"And your hair. Brush it back so we can see your lovely face." Jillian grabbed her daughter's wrist despite the protests. "Come. I'll show you what I mean. Everett Bruce may show up, you know."

"So?" Norma, said, looking back at Angel with a "please help me" look as her mother tugged her up the stairs.

Angel shrugged, mouthed the word *sorry* to Norma. They both knew that there was no changing Jillian's mind once it fixed on something. And at that moment she was intensely fixed on getting her daughter to be what she considered presentable for Mr. Bruce. That was if he even bothered to show up. The invitation had been extended to him only two days earlier and from what Jillian had said when the family returned from Nancy's Wednesday night, he would try to make it but couldn't promise. To Angel's way of thinking, that was likely a polite way of saying no. But she didn't have time to dwell on that as she began to remove the husks from the corn. The soup would have to chill in the refrigerator and needed to go on now. She had a million things to do to get the mise en place done by the time the other chefs arrived.

A few hours later, Angel and the two temporary chefs were quickly but carefully dishing soup into bowls and topping them with lobster salad. A trio of waiters carried the food out to the nearly one hundred guests seated at tables of eight on the lawn. The weather had cooperated for the most part, turning cloudy but bright with no rain just before the guests started to arrive. Yet it was obvious to Angel, and everyone who lived in the household, that Jillian was deeply disappointed, despite presenting big smiles and a cheerful voice. The most desired guest had not showed up, and to Jillian it would have meant the world to have Everett Bruce at her gathering. Even Irvin had talked about being impressed with Mr. Bruce's many accomplishments at dinner the previous night. Still, Jillian hadn't given up hope entirely, Angel noted. She kept looking up and down the blocks where all the cars were parked. Or glancing at her watch.

And then suddenly the mood shifted, palpably. Whisperings of a silvery convertible Maserati pulling up floated about. The doorbell rang and both Jillian and Irvin appeared in the foyer out of nowhere to answer it. Angel couldn't see the Harrisons or the newly arrived guest from her station in the kitchen, but she could hear the three of them chatting as they made their way across the great room toward the French doors leading out to the lawn. Angel assumed this was Everett Bruce, since seasoned guests knew to enter from the gate at the side of the lawn.

The picture window in the kitchen presented a bird's-eye view of the festivities. Angel, her curiosity piqued by all the excitement in the air, looked up from a platter she was preparing, hoping to catch a glimpse of the esteemed one. She got only a side view but was surprised that he seemed oddly familiar. Her eyes followed as the Harrisons introduced him to a small group. She hoped that he would turn to face the kitchen window, but Jillian led him even farther away. So Angel got back to work, soon forgetting all about him as she supervised the steady progression of food and beverages to and from the party. It was going to be a long day; her feet were already starting to ache.

Several hours later she busily assembled the last of many platters with a variety of cheeses and the fresh-baked sourdough bread she had picked up that morning. The guests would stay on for at least another hour, but their numbers had begun to dwindle, and she had finally found a moment to sit and rest her tired feet at the kitchen table when she heard voices in the great room beside the kitchen. She jumped up just as Jillian stuck her head through the kitchen doorway. "Angel, a few of us are headed for the parlor. Make up a couple more of those cheese platters and bring up two bottles of pinot noir from the cellar, will you?"

"Of course, Mrs. Harrison." As her employer hurried off, Angel let out a weary breath, then walked to a cabinet and reached for two additional platters. So much for resting her exhausted bones. That luxury would have to wait.

"My compliments to the chef."

The deep voice startled her. She had thought she was alone in the kitchen; she had sent one of the temporary chefs down to the cellar to fetch the wine, and the rest of the help was out on the lawn, beginning to clean up. Her hands were covered in soap suds as she twisted around to face a tall, handsome man standing behind her. Not many guests took the time to acknowledge the chef at affairs like this. "Thank you," she said. "I appreciate that."

"It was all nicely done. I really enjoyed the seafood and soup." He lifted his half-full wineglass in a salute toward her.

"Yes, Angel does a fantastic job," Jillian said, popping back into the kitchen behind him.

"You look familiar," the man said to Angel, a slight frown creasing his forehead. "Have we met? At an event somewhere?"

Angel seriously doubted she'd met one of Jillian's friends unless it was in a serving capacity. They were an entirely different class of people, mountains apart. She scoffed softly. "I don't think so."

"I'm almost sure we have, and it was recent. Maybe at a restaurant around here."

That's when it clicked for Angel. This was the man she had run into at Nancy's the other day. The one who'd picked her pad up from the floor. He'd been wearing a hat then. But for the first time today she took note of the graying hair, the husky voice. So the man she had met earlier that week and this eagerly anticipated guest, Everett Bruce, were one and the same. What were the odds?

Everything seemed to click at that moment for him, too. "The restaurant on the water," he said, pointing at her with recognition. "I picked up your notepad with recipes, right?"

"Yes," Angel said, smiling. "I remember now." She couldn't believe the coincidence. She had assumed a man with the reputation of Everett Bruce would be more pretentious, more difficult, more like her boss. But he seemed easygoing and friendly. Not at all what Angel would have expected. Of course, she had been around him only a few short moments. In her experience, people could be as fickle as the weather and change on you without warning.

"Um, excuse me," Jillian said, clearing her throat. "You two have met, Everett?"

"Only momentarily," he said. "We ran into each other at Nancy's a couple of days ago."

"Oh, really?" Jillian said. She eyed Angel sharply. "You should have told me you met him."

"I had no idea who he was then," Angel added, the smile quickly falling from her face.

"And I had no idea you were a chef," Everett said. "Now I get it. How are the recipes coming?"

Angel could almost feel the heat emanating from Jillian's flashing eyes. "Um, just fine," she said, anxiously wiping her hands on the cloth towel at her waist. She picked up a knife and began to slice some Gruyère cheese, hoping he would drop the chatter. That had been more than enough friendly banter with one of the guests. Especially *this* guest.

Angel was actually relieved to see Jillian tug at Everett's sleeve out of the corner of her eye. "Let's come along," Jillian said, her expression softening. "The others are in the parlor waiting."

When the two strolled off together, Angel breathed a sigh of relief. For now. But she was certain that was not the end of it. She would hear more about this whole episode later from Jillian.

Not ten minutes had passed after the last guests said their goodbyes when Jillian marched into the kitchen, followed by Irvin, who announced that he was heading to the tennis court for a late match. "Another fine meal, Angel," he said, and took off.

Norma retreated to her room with a novel. Angel braced herself as she and the two other chefs finished tidying up the kitchen.

"I cannot believe you met him and never said a word to me, Angel." Jillian stood directly across the countertop, one hand on her hip.

Angel had hoped—foolishly perhaps—that Jillian would at least wait until the temporary help departed before starting in on her. Or pulled her aside. This was going to be humiliating. But not surprising. Jillian had done this in front of others before. Usually, it was over a dish not prepared to her liking—pasta a little overcooked, dessert much too sweet, the wine not coming fast enough.

"We kind of bumped into each other at the restaurant," Angel said softly. "How was I to know it was him?"

"I described him to you before you left. I distinctly told you to let me know if he was there."

"You did, but honestly, the description you gave could have fit a lot of older Black men. And I was so focused on getting the table for you. The thought that he could have been Mr. Bruce never entered my mind." Angel really wanted to ask Jillian what difference it would have made even if she *had* recognized him and texted or called to alert her boss. Absolutely none. Not one bit of difference.

"And what's this about some soup?" Jillian practically spit the words out.

Angel stiffened as the other two chefs moved away to create some distance. She had expected the question and had her response ready. "Oh, I jotted down some notes and recipes for things I was preparing for the party on a pad I keep in my purse. I dropped it and Mr. Bruce picked it up. That's all. Only I didn't know it was him then, of course." She wasn't ready to tell Jillian that she was working on a cookbook. Maybe never would be. No telling how she would react to that news.

Angel could feel her boss watching her closely as she packed leftovers from a tray into smaller dishes. She was being sized up, evaluated, judged. Still, she kept quiet. She knew from experience that this was the moment to keep her mouth shut. The first time Jillian had gotten on Angel about something in front of others, she'd staunchly defended herself and there was a lengthy heated exchange. Angel had been certain she was about to lose her job when Jillian yelled at the top of her lungs and told Angel to get out of her sight. Fortunately, by the following morning they had both cooled down and Jillian carried on as if nothing had happened. But Angel decided then and there never to challenge her boss again. She had far more to lose in any kind of skirmish than Jillian did.

"I'll let it go this time," Jillian said finally. "But see that nothing like this ever happens again. I have to be able to trust you, Angel."

She nodded. "Understood."

"I should hope so. As you know, tomorrow we're all taking the ferry over to Nantucket to spend the day with friends. What are your plans?"

Thank goodness the nasty little exchange was over; Jillian seemed ready to move on. "If the weather's nice, I'll probably walk to the beach."

"Sounds lovely. Just be sure to lock up."

3

Only blocks into the two-and-a-half-mile walk to the beach, Angel began to regret her decision. The blazing-hot sun pounded relentlessly on her bare shoulders and back, clad only in a white cotton sundress with spaghetti straps. The big, floppy straw hat that she'd almost left behind wasn't helping much. This was one of those scorching August days that made any kind of strenuous activity almost unbearable, no matter how lightly one dressed. But she had come too far to turn back now. She shifted her canvas beach bag—feeling like it weighed a ton—and a large sketch pad from one arm to the other, staring with envy as one air-conditioned car after another whizzed by.

Normally this path along Seaview Avenue was so well traveled that pedestrians had to weave in and out to avoid one another and those biking. Today it seemed that she was one of only a few souls brave enough to defy this heat, or foolish enough, depending on how you looked at it. But she loved the beach so much, had ever since the days she'd visited the island every summer with her parents. She got so little time off to enjoy it; she had to take advantage of every opportunity.

The lukewarm gust of air that fluttered up from the wide-open ocean to her left felt heaven-sent. She squinted across the water toward the boats in the distance, as visions of lounging on the sand near the ocean breezes, sketching the scenery, and dipping her toes into the cool waters propelled her forward.

Her vision soon shifted back to the avenue where a silver convertible with the top down cruised by. Not sure she would have made that choice today, she thought, frowning at the car. Too much damn sun. When the vehicle slowed and swerved abruptly to the side of the road just ahead, it dawned on her that it was a Maserati. The driver twisted in his seat and waved, and she realized it was Everett Bruce. Angel looked behind her, thinking that he must have stopped for someone else. No way he was waiting for her. But there was no one there. He waved again. She checked behind again. It would be beyond embarrassing to run up to the car only to be told he had stopped for some other reason, not for her. So she kept her pace. As she got closer, the wave turned into a beckoning finger; his eyes were looking directly at her.

She walked faster and just as she approached the car, he leaned over and the passenger-side door swung open. "Can I give you a lift?"

He said it as if it were the most ordinary thing in the world for a man like him to offer a ride to a woman like her. It almost took her breath away but she kept her composure. "I'm heading for the beach."

"The beach just up the way on the left?"

She nodded, feeling silly. She should have been clearer. There were dozens of public and private beaches on the island.

"Hop on in," he said as the trunk popped up. "I'll drop you off."

She tossed her bag and sketch pad into the trunk and sank into the soft leather seat beside him. "Thank you so much for stopping," she said, holding on to her hat as he roared off.

"My pleasure. It's pretty hot to be out there walking today. Actually, it's kind of hot for the beach."

She smiled. "I agree it's too hot for all this walking but it's never too hot for the beach. The hotter, the better."

He chuckled. "Oh, really? To each his own, I guess. Or her."

"I could say the same thing about having the top down on a day like this instead of turning on the air."

He shook his head. "Nope. It's never too hot to have the top down. Feel that ocean breeze. Although I'm no fan of the beach or sand."

"I have to admit this does feel nice. Cooler than I expected." She removed her hat and lifted her face to let the breeze cool her off. "I can't help but wonder if you don't like the beach why you decided to come to an island."

"Fair enough. I was here several years ago. Loved everything else about it. The people, the vibe, the food. Always wanted to come back. So when friends offered their house to me, I took them up on it."

"You have some nice friends."

He laughed and nodded. "I agree."

"I've only been in a convertible once before."

"You don't see them as much as you used to."

Especially not one like this, she was tempted to say but simply nodded. "I remember the last time clearly because this sudden downpour hit us out of nowhere."

"That happened here?"

"No. Washington, DC."

"Oh, okay. That's where you live?"

"Yes. What about you?" Jillian had mentioned that he had a place in Maryland, but she didn't want to let on that she already knew this. Then again, he probably had more than one house, and that might not be his primary residence.

"Potomac, Maryland," he said. "Not far outside of DC. But I was born in a small town in Virginia that you've probably never heard of. Ruckersville."

"Ruckersville? Can't say I have."

He chuckled. "Very rural, especially back then. Closest town you've probably heard of is Charlottesville."

She nodded with recognition. "How does one go from a small rural town to Potomac, Maryland?"

"A lot of hard work with a tiny bit of luck. I got a full scholarship for college at UVA, then went on to business school. Cultivated some good connections along the way, many I'm still in touch with today."

She listened in silence as he spoke, the ocean on the left, a large pond on the right. She could tell that he was very comfortable discussing his business accomplishments. His expression was serious, though not sad. He was fit and good-looking in an understated way, with a smooth, dark complexion. His neatly trimmed hair, mustache, and beard all showed hints of gray. She stole another glimpse of his profile out of the corner of her eye, found herself wondering what his wife may have been like and whether he still missed her. From what Jillian had said, it had been only a year since her sudden death.

When they came to Jaws Bridge just as they crossed from Oak Bluffs into Edgartown, her attention turned to the line of teens perched on the edge of the railing, all looking ready to dive straight into the ocean.

"Young people," he said, shaking his head with disapproval.

"I know." She chuckled. "But I probably would have done the same thing myself when I was that age."

Everett gave her a sideways glance. "The sign up there specifically says no jumping or diving."

She shrugged. "Still, it looks like fun. You remember how it was when you were a kid. We took more risks."

He shook his head firmly. "Not life-threatening risks. Looks dangerous."

"That's part of the thrill for them. You're right though. Two people did drown not long ago. They were brothers."

"That's unfortunate, but it was bound to happen."

She nodded in agreement.

He pulled into a small parking spot near the beach and smiled at her. "I hope you have plenty of sunblock. The sun is intense today."

She slipped her hat back on and reached for the door handle. "I know. It's so humid I probably won't stay long. Just get wet and head back shortly. I really appreciate the lift."

"No problem. I'm headed to a gallery in Edgartown. Would have passed by here anyway."

"That should be fun. I love art," she blurted excitedly, ready to tell him about her love of drawing. Then she realized with embarrassment that he might think she was looking for an invitation to join him.

"I noticed the sketch pad," he said, nodding.

"Mm-hmm," she said. "My other passion."

He lifted his eyebrows quizzically.

"Besides cooking."

"Ah, yes," he said.

This was beginning to feel awkward. She opened the car door. "Well, thanks again for the ride."

"Hold up. Would you care to join me? There's a new exhibit this week. You'd probably like it."

She blinked, caught totally off guard. He was probably being considerate, not really expecting her to say yes. "Um, that's so nice but you've done enough. I don't want to trouble you with having to bring me back."

"It's no trouble, really."

"Really?" She looked down at her flip-flops, then over at his collared white shirt. "I'm not dressed right. This is too causal for a . . ."

He shrugged. "You look nice. It's the beach. Everyone is casual."

She paused. The cool refines of an air-conditioned gallery sounded extremely tempting on this ninety-five-degree day. Yes, she was underdressed compared to him but like he'd said, this was on an island. There were bound to be people there dressed in a more relaxed style.

"But it's up to you," he said. "I wouldn't want you to feel uncomfortable."

"If you think I look okay, then maybe . . ."

"You look fine."

"Okay, yes, I'd love to go," she said, shutting the door.

He smiled and she gripped her hat as he sped off.

* * *

They chatted nonstop until he pulled into a parking lot near the gallery. It was obvious from the moment they stepped inside and were greeted by a woman who Angel assumed was the owner or manager that not only was Everett well-known, but he was also well-liked. The slender red-haired woman, dressed in all white with a colorful scarf draped around her shoulders, fussed about, flattering him every chance she got. *You look wonderful, Mr. Bruce. Your taste in artwork is impeccable. The gallery can't thank you enough for your generosity.* And on and on she went.

So Everett was supporting the gallery somehow. He smiled quietly as the woman continued, but in the very short time she'd been around him, Angel surmised that he would happily do without all the praise and was simply being polite. Finally, during a brief lull in the conversation, Everett introduced her to Angel as the gallery owner. Jackie Anderson was courteous enough, smiling as she and Angel shook hands in greeting. Still, Angel could detect an ever-so-slight air of condescension as Jackie adroitly sized her up, from the well-worn flip-flops to the dime-store straw hat. Jackie soon turned her attention back to Everett, and Angel quietly slipped away to check out the artwork.

She had gotten lost while examining the seascape paintings when a young Black man in his thirties approached her. He was medium height and medium complexioned, with a medium build. "You really seem into all this," he said, a slight smile playing around his lips as he watched her.

She nodded. "He's very good, this Reggie Hawthorne," she said, peering closely at the artist name tag next to the dark seascape that she had been admiring. "There's something haunting, even a little scary, about his work. The menacing way the waves are drawn makes you feel like you're about to be swallowed by the sea. Gives me chills." She paused and turned to face the man. "What do you think?"

"I think I agree with you. I enjoy this work, too." He extended his hand. "Reggie Hawthorne."

She gasped and laughed as they shook. "Oh. I don't usually get to meet the artist in the flesh, Mr. Hawthorne."

"Reggie, please. And you, who so nicely admired my work, are?"

"Angel Gibson." She hoped she wasn't blushing. Maybe she had been overly effusive. "I haven't said too much, have I?"

"Not at all. It's refreshing to hear raw praise that doesn't seem calculated to sound impressive. Are you an artist?"

She shook her head shyly. "Not really. I mean, I love to sketch but . . ."

"Then you're an artist. What do you draw?"

"Landscapes. Some portraits." She looked up toward one of his paintings. "Nothing even half as good as all this, though."

"Don't be so hard on yourself. Your work is probably better than you believe it to be."

She smiled just as Everett approached, sans Jackie, bearing a stern expression she had not seen before on his face. It was puzzling, and she didn't know what to think.

"Definitely was not expecting to see you here," Everett said, gritting his teeth as he cast a sharp glance toward Reggie.

Reggie shrugged. "Plans change, man."

"So Jackie just explained."

Reggie's eyes darted back and forth between Angel and Everett. "Are the two of you together?"

"Yes," Everett said pointedly.

Reggie shoved both hands into his pockets. "I see."

As this somewhat terse exchange unfolded, it did not escape Angel's notice that the two hadn't shaken hands, that there was no warmth between them. She shifted from one foot to the other, growing more uneasy by the minute. "I was just admiring his artwork," Angel said.

Everett nodded stiffly. "Ready to get out of here?"

"Um, yes. Whenever you are." All so odd, she thought as Reggie turned his back to them and they walked away. But she felt relieved to get out of there, given the obvious bad blood between the two of them.

Just as they approached the entrance, Everett paused. "Give me a minute," he said, and Angel watched anxiously as he headed into the crowd, thinking he might make his way back to have a few private words with Reggie. Instead, he approached Jackie. The two slipped off, stopping near a far corner, and were soon in the midst of an animated exchange, Everett doing most of the talking. Angel stared, startled. His behavior was uncomfortable to witness.

Everett made his way toward the entrance and opened the door for her. They descended the stairs and silently made their way past the boutiques and cafés on the busy streets of Edgartown, heading toward his car. He walked so fast she could barely keep up with him. What had transpired back there in the gallery?

"Is everything all right?" she asked, trying to break the awkward silence and curious about what had set him off.

"Everything is fine." He slowed down and forced a smile. "Would you like to get a bite to eat before I take you back?"

Everything was very obviously *not* so fine, she thought. At least it hadn't been a moment ago. Even though he had been nothing but kind and generous toward her, she did not feel she knew him well enough to pry further if he was disinclined to open up, especially now that she had seen a flash of his temper.

She shook her head. "Thanks, but no. I really should get back and start on dinner. The Harrisons will be returning soon."

"I understand. Maybe another time."

Another time? Angel wondered about that. She wasn't sure she wanted there to be another time after what she'd just seen and heard.

4

Angel muttered to herself as she opened the front door of the Harrison household to the sound of voices. She had hoped to slip back in before the family returned from their outing to Nantucket with time to shower, change, and get started on dinner. They would all be famished after spending a blistering day walking along Main Street, visiting the perfumery, boutiques, and galleries. They'd likely had lunch at the home of friends who had property on the island, but would expect dinner soon.

As she stepped into the foyer and removed her hat, her cell phone buzzed. She glanced down to see a text message from Jillian.

We got back twenty minutes ago. Where are you?

Angel could feel the impatience emanating from the words on her screen. She glanced at the time on her phone: it was approaching four o'clock. Where had the hours gone since she'd slipped into Everett's car that afternoon? It had been a whirlwind of a day with the minutes whizzing by. During the ride from the gallery, Everett apologized twice for his brusque behavior, quickly reverting to his charming and considerate self. Although she was still deeply puzzled as to what might have provoked such an abrupt change in him, his apology had put her mind at ease. He'd even taken a circuitous route through the side streets behind the house so they could have a little extra time to chat. By the time she alighted from his car and he sped off, she'd felt much better about their day together and their budding friendship.

"So there you are," Irvin said, his tanned face peering up from the couch, his hand holding a goblet full of red wine.

Angel paused beneath the arched entrance to the parlor. The complexions of the entire family had turned a warm tawny shade after a day spent in the sun. "How was Nantucket?"

Jillian stood in the bay window on the far side of the room, surrounded by several shopping bags of all sizes. "Oh, it was fine."

Angel nodded. She had decided not to tell them that she'd actually spent the afternoon hanging out with Everett Bruce. She had a pretty good feeling that such news was better left unsaid.

Norma hopped up from her seat beside her dad and grabbed a shopping bag from the bookstore in Nantucket off the coffee table. "Did you get much drawing done on the beach?" she asked as she headed for the stairs.

"No. Not really," Angel said.

"It was probably too hot," Irvin said.

"We barely spent an hour shopping," Norma added, "before we went to Ray and Ruth's house."

"Your mother still managed to spend a small fortune," Irvin said, eyeing his wife as she sorted through all her recent purchases.

"Were you at the beach all that time, Angel?" Jillian asked.

"Um, yes. For the most part."

"Really?" Jillian said. "You were out in that hot sun all day long? How could you stand it?"

"I spent a lot of time cooling down in the water," Angel said, avoiding Jillian's gaze. In an attempt to change the subject, she was about to comment on how much cooler it used to be when she'd visited the island every year with her parents, but her cell phone beeped. She glanced down thinking it was one of her friends in DC only to glimpse the beginning of a text message from Everett. So soon? "Well, I should get started on dinner."

"Yes, you should," Jillian said.

"Salmon tonight?" Irvin asked.

Angel nodded. "With that lemon-and-caper butter sauce you like. Just need to freshen up first."

She darted up the stairs, reading the message. He was checking to make sure everything had worked out for her, given that she was worried about getting dinner started in time. How considerate. She texted back explaining that the Harrisons were already there when she arrived but that all was well. He then asked her out for lunch the following afternoon. She was surprised but quickly accepted, feeling flattered that he wanted to spend more time with her. Gene crossed her mind but she didn't feel it would be cheating. She and Gene had barely corresponded since she'd left DC, and it was usually her reaching out to him. Anyway, she and Everett were simply a couple of friends going out for a bite to eat.

She hopped into the shower. She was surprised that she had enjoyed his company so much; she usually went for the musical or artsy types, like Gene and Reggie. But Everett's being a wildly successful businessman was a big reason why she had reconsidered and decided to overlook the flare-up at the gallery. It was understandable, even to be expected, that he would have a tough side to him. No one, especially a Black man, could have made it as far as he had by being a softy all the time. Besides, she found it exciting to step outside her box and spend time with someone so different from what she was used to. She worked hard when she was there, cooking and shopping for the Harrisons and occasionally for other local families for special events. She deserved to have some fun.

Now all she had to do was figure out what to tell the Harrisons to get a few hours away tomorrow afternoon. As far as she knew, they had no special plans, and the weather was expected to be more pleasant after showers tonight. She would prepare a light lunch of a cold pasta-and-chicken salad with croutons made from the sourdough bread left over from yesterday's party, along with the mojito cocktails that Irvin loved. She would present it all especially nicely on one of the screened porches, where they would have a relaxed, picturesque view of the ocean while they dined.

* * *

After the Harrisons had downed a few drinks with lunch the following afternoon, Angel told the family she was going to catch the bus into Edgartown to do a little shopping. She hated lying but sometimes a little fibbing was necessary to keep the peace. No telling how Jillian would react if told that her private chef was spending all this time with a cherished idol of hers. Irvin, bless his heart, held out the keys to the Benz. "Go ahead, take the car," he said. "We won't need it. Or at least I won't." He glanced at Jillian, as if to double-check. Jillian was quiet for a moment as she sipped her cocktail, then nodded. "As long as you have it back by five. I need it for my book club meeting tonight."

"Oh, thank you, but I'm fine with getting the bus. It's such a nice day." She slipped out the door and darted to the end of the block where Everett was waiting. Meeting around the corner did not seem strange at all to him since no parking was allowed in front of the house.

The ride back to Edgartown with Everett was every bit as enjoyable as it had been the day before. This time she was dressed more appropriately, wearing a little makeup, a sundress, and cute sandals. The seafood restaurant, right on the water, had a magnificent view of the sea and sky as well as the quaint little ferry that chugged the short distance back and forth to Chappaquiddick Island. They ordered oysters on the half shell, lobsters, and Bloody Marys, then sat for two hours discussing art, vacationing on the island, and food—including their mutual fondness for soup of all kinds, from chowders to stews. She caught glimpses of a geeky side emerging as he readily discussed his business and charitable giving. It was all a refreshing change from some of the slick guys she'd dated in the past.

When he reminded her that this was only his second time visiting Martha's Vineyard, she told him all about how her family used to vacation there every year when she was a small child. She described what had changed about the island since then, and what remained the same. She even divulged a little about what it had been like when her mom deserted the family after their last visit, something she seldom shared with anyone she had recently met. But Everett was attentive, nonjudgmental, and surprisingly easy to talk to.

"That must have been difficult," he said softly. "How old were you when it happened?"

"About twelve."

"A very sensitive age."

"Mama came back into the picture a year after their divorce became final. She had remarried by then and moved to Richmond, Virginia. I became really close to my father when it was just the two of us. He's the one who got me interested in cooking. He owned two seafood restaurants in Maryland." She shrugged. "Until he lost them."

"Oh, wow. What happened?"

"He never talked about it much. All I know is that it had something to do with a shady partner."

Everett shook his head. "That sounds unfortunate."

"Yeah. But he went on to teach and got me to study culinary arts."

"I can sense your affection and admiration for him," Everett said, smiling at her. "Where is your dad now?"

"He passed away, almost ten years ago now."

"Sorry to hear that."

"And then my mother, she and her husband were killed in a car crash two years later."

"Good grief," Everett said, clearly stricken. "I'm so sorry."

She leaned in slightly, spoke softly. "I feel like an orphan now. But that's life. You take it as it comes, and it isn't always pretty."

"You've done very well for yourself. A personal chef working here in paradise. And you said you just bought a condo in DC?"

She nodded. "I try."

"I know what you mean about feeling like an orphan, though. My mother passed away a few years ago. She was my rock. Never knew my father."

"I'm so sorry to hear that."

He chuckled softly. "We're both full of sorrys today, aren't we?"

She smiled. "Guess we are."

"Tell me, are you seeing anyone special?"

"Um, not really. We just broke up." Not entirely the truth. But for some reason she didn't want Everett to know she was in a relationship, even a bad one. He might decide to stop spending time with her if he thought she had a boyfriend back home. And she really enjoyed his company.

"I see. Are you okay with that?" he asked.

"I'm fine with it. It's probably time for us to move on." The more time she spent away from Gene and with Everett, the more true that felt. She deserved someone who would treat her better than Gene did. "Do you have any siblings?" It was also time to move on to another topic.

"An older sister named Ida. Three years older."

"Married?"

"No, she lives on the estate, as a matter of fact."

"Oh."

"Helps me manage my place in Potomac. That's where I spend most of my time."

Angel nodded, trying to visualize a place grand enough to need a manager. "What's it like there?"

"Very tranquil. It's several acres with gardens, woods, a few buildings. The river runs along the back edge. Not that huge but I'm away a lot. She's a big help."

She smiled to herself. They obviously had different definitions of *huge*. At least when it came to property. All very interesting.

What she was most curious about though was his late wife and the mystery surrounding her sudden death. How had it happened? What had their life together been like? She had many questions but for some reason didn't feel comfortable broaching the topic outright.

"I've never been married," she volunteered, hoping that offering the information would encourage him to open up about his own previous marital status.

"Interesting." he said, suddenly beginning to focus intently on breaking up his lobster.

That was it? That was all he had to say? "I guess," she said.

"Well, you're still young."

"I'm thirty-three."

"Then you don't look your age."

"Thank you."

"You have plenty of time to think about marriage."

He was not going to make this easy. "Um, what about you?"

"Me? I'm forty-five."

"I meant . . ." She paused and looked at him closely. He was still fiddling with his lobster. He had to have known that was *not* what she'd meant. It felt to her like he was pulling back from the free exchange they'd been engaging in up to now. "Weren't you married at one time?" There. She'd said it. She had asked the burning question. But she regretted it almost immediately. The taut expression, the gritting of the teeth that she hadn't seen since yesterday at the gallery startled her. He wiped his fingers on his napkin, then looked at her pointedly. She held her fork in midair, waiting.

He cleared his throat, softened his expression to something that read: okay, let's get this over with. "Yes. Chloe and I were married for almost four years."

So that was her name. Chloe. Angel nodded, hoping for more. It wasn't coming. "What happened?" she finally asked.

His downward glance shielded his brown eyes. "She passed away suddenly, about a year ago."

"I'm really sorry about that."

His eyes came back to her and she sensed his sadness. He shrugged.

"What was she . . . Chloe . . . like? Are you okay to talk about it?"

"Not really but I understand why people are curious. She was beautiful," he said matter-of-factly as he chewed his lobster. "Almost too beautiful."

"*Too* beautiful? Whatever does that mean?"

He forced a slight smile. "I'll leave that to your interpretation. Also adventurous, insatiable when it came to living life."

"How so, if you don't mind me asking?"

"I think I've said enough. At least for now. Too many fresh memories."

She nodded, leaned back in her seat. "I understand." Or she was trying to. There was so much more she wanted to know. Was his reluctance due to the sudden circumstances surrounding her death? Or did he still have feelings for her? Or both? He obviously had found her extremely attractive. Now Angel found herself wondering where he thought she fell on the looks spectrum. Did he think she was pretty?

Stop it, she admonished herself. Stop comparing yourself to his late wife. She and Everett were just friends. Chloe had been his wife. Of course he had special feelings for her.

She excused herself to use the restroom, to give them both time to recover from the tense exchange. She really needed a moment to get her head together. Studying her face in the mirror as she washed her hands, she let out a deep breath. *Angel, it's earth calling. Get your head out of the clouds and back down here where it belongs. He's a freaking billionaire. He isn't interested in you in that way. He's just in need of companionship while here on the island.* He probably found her fresh, entertaining. They enjoyed each other's company. After the summer they would go back to their routines. She to her drummer boyfriend named Gene. He to his megadigs in Potomac. That was it. That would always be it.

5

An hour here. A few hours there. That was all the time Angel could manage to steal away. Her moments with Everett were limited to lunch, quick gallery runs, visits to nearby attractions. One activity every few days, never more than that. Such was her life as a personal chef for a family that expected her to serve and wait on them pretty much around the clock during the month of August.

She was able to slip back out for a couple of drinks with Everett one evening during her final week there; Irvin and Jillian were attending a gathering at a friend's house in Chilmark. Earlier that day, she and Everett had toured a nearby lighthouse in Edgartown overlooking the harbor, where they climbed the stairs to take in the magnificent view. Then they did a quick drive past the East Chop Lighthouse before he dropped her back at the house. That night, over drinks, it dawned on them both that this was the first and only time they had been in each other's company after dark.

"We need to figure out how to get you out for more than a

few hours at a time. Before you leave, I want to take a drive to Menemsha to sit on the beach and watch the sun go down. You've talked about it so much."

"Yes, you really have to see it, even if I can't go with you. Just make sure to allow plenty of time to get there. Parking is a nightmare, and you want to have time to pick up some fresh seafood at the fish markets in the village along the way to the beach."

"What's the fun in going without you? You're not going to let me drive all the way down there to watch what you describe as a mesmerizing, blazing-red sunset all alone, are you?"

She smiled with regret. "I would love to join you, Everett, but I might not be able to get away. Ideally you leave around five or six on a day when the weather is clear. That's when I'm preparing dinner."

"You go back to DC on Saturday, right? That leaves tomorrow, Thursday, and Friday." He picked up his cell phone. "The forecast for tomorrow is sunny. Thursday, it might rain. I doubt you'd want to go the day before you leave. So, looks like tomorrow is our best bet."

"Tomorrow won't work. Not enough of a heads-up for them."

He shook his head. "I'm really surprised you can't get more time off. Seems unfair."

She shrugged. "I get enough, you know. Half a day on Sundays. And they're pretty flexible about letting me have a day here and there as long as it doesn't interfere with their plans and I give plenty of notice."

"The weather isn't always going to cooperate on Sundays just so you can go to Menemsha or do other outdoor activities in the evening."

"True." An occasional afternoon off to shop for herself had seemed like enough until now. Meeting Everett had changed things. She wanted to spend more time with him during the few days they had left, but there wasn't much she could do about it.

"Tell them it's some kind of chef's convention or a night cooking class."

She shook her head. "I've never done anything like that before. Mrs. Harrison would have a million questions. And she has a lot of contacts on the island. She could easily find out that there's no such thing."

As much as she enjoyed spending time with him, she didn't want to risk getting caught in a lie and perhaps lose her job and the opportunity to visit the island, all expenses paid, every summer. Not worth it for a man and a relationship that would never grow into anything more than friendship. She couldn't even be sure they would remain friends once they both went back home. They lived such different lifestyles.

"I don't think that would fly with them," she continued. "Too chancy."

"I get it," he said softly. "That's one of the things I admire about you, sticking to what's important to you regardless. Like your work."

She nodded in appreciation. She suspected that not many women turned down opportunities to spend time with this man. Especially sitting on the beach watching the sun go down.

He smiled, reached across the table to take her hand. He squeezed tightly, tenderly. She definitely had not expected anything like that. It took her completely by surprise; she wasn't sure what to think. Was he being romantic? If so, this was a first. A warm, fuzzy feeling spread through her body as they sat in silence for a few minutes. His hand never left hers.

"Maybe I could just tell them the truth," she said finally. "Or at least, partly."

He raised an eyebrow. "I thought we weren't going to chance you losing a job you love."

No, she didn't want to lose her job. But he was sitting there across from her holding her hand affectionately. The feelings for him that she'd learned to bury now came bubbling to the surface. "The biggest risk would be in telling them who I've been spending my time with. Like I told you, Jillian Harrison is a huge admirer of yours. She would not be happy finding out I hid our friendship from her."

He nodded with understanding. "She did seem to have ideas about me dating her daughter, even though her daughter never expressed any interest."

"You probably get that a lot," she said.

"You have no idea. But I understand. Mothers are looking after their daughters. Can't blame them for that. They seem to think I'm a catch."

"Because you are, silly."

"Do *you* think that? I hope so."

Now she was certain he was coming on to her. She liked it. She just prayed she wasn't blushing. "Maybe," she said, smiling coyly.

He leaned in over his martini, a conspiratorial expression playing around his eyes. "They don't know about the bodies in the backyard."

She froze for a second. "Excuse me?"

"The mothers and their daughters."

She laughed lightly as he chuckled at his own joke. "Stop it," she said. "Not funny, you know."

"I'm kidding," he said. Then his tone became more serious. "You were suggesting telling them the truth."

She nodded. "I could say I'm going out with someone. Just not who it is. Like a friend visiting from DC."

"Would that work?"

"Maybe."

"Okay. So, Menemsha tomorrow is sounding more and more like a possibility, then?"

"Like I said, maybe." She was certainly going to give it a try. She was a little nervous about the whole idea but really wanted more time with Everett before returning to DC, to see where this might go. "I'll text you tonight to confirm."

"I hate that you have to deal with this just for a night out with me. But you leave this weekend. Then I'm off to Europe on business for several weeks when I leave here in mid-September."

She smiled at the way he said that so nonchalantly. As if zipping off to Europe for a lengthy stay were the most ordinary thing a person could do, even a businessman. He led a charmed life.

"Anything I can do to help?" he asked. "If so, just let me know."

She shook her head. "Leave it to me." The less he was involved in this, the better. Best she face Jillian alone.

"Well, good luck. I'm rooting for you and for us spending time together tomorrow night."

* * *

Jillian and Irvin were still out when Angel returned to the house around ten that night, so she sat up in bed and tried to read a novel while waiting. Unable to concentrate on a single sentence, she practiced in her head exactly what she would say to her employer.

"Mrs. Harrison, a friend is having some people over tomorrow. Is it okay if I leave something for you all to warm up for dinner?"

Or maybe she should be more direct: "A friend is visiting from DC and wants to meet up for dinner tomorrow. I'll leave dinner for you all to heat up when you're ready to eat."

Angel stopped, tried to clear her mind. Here she was rehearsing what to say to get a night out on her own, as if she were a child. She worked her butt off for the Harrisons for the entire month of

August. Getting half a day off shouldn't be such a big deal if the family had nothing special going on. She picked her novel back up, determined to focus on reading until they got home.

When they still had not returned by eleven, she decided that this was going to have to wait until morning. It was already too late to approach them tonight. Disappointing, but not a darn thing she could do about it. She sent a text to Everett to update him, then turned off the lights.

The next thing Angel knew, someone was calling her name from a distance. The voice was pulling her out of a restless slumber and a recurring dream that hadn't invaded her sleep in many years. It was almost pitch-black; she was running, running, running through a dense fog while glancing back repeatedly over her shoulder to see if anyone was still following.

Groggy, she forced her eyelids open, her stomach in knots, and squinted in the dark at the bright-red neon numbers on her digital clock. It was 12:40 a.m., less than two hours since she'd turned off the lights. She sat up as the voice called her name again, and she immediately recognized it as Jillian. Angel frowned and quickly slid into her bathrobe, wondering what could possibly be so urgent at this hour. She couldn't ever remember being woken in the middle of the night since she'd been employed by the Harrisons.

She skipped breathlessly down the stairs and rushed into the parlor to find Jillian standing near a window. She was alone; Angel assumed that Irvin and Norma had gone to bed. Whatever the big problem was, it had not been significant enough to keep the two of them up. Angel relaxed a bit.

"Yes, Mrs. Harrison. Is everything all right?"

Jillian greeted her with an icy glare. Angel feared that maybe she'd started to relax too soon. The knots returned to her stomach, tighter than ever.

"I know all about what you've been up to, pretending you're

going to the beach or out shopping. You think you're clever, don't you?"

Angel swallowed hard. Was this really happening? Did it mean what she thought? That Mrs. Harrison knew she had been spending time with Everett Bruce? Lots of time. She cleared her throat. "Excuse me?"

"Oh, don't give me that doe-eyed, innocent look. You aren't fooling me for a minute."

"I have no idea what you're talking about, Mrs. Harrison." This was the last thing Angel had expected right now, and she had no idea how to react. Her gut reaction was to deny, deny, deny. She needed time to gather her thoughts.

"You know exactly what I mean. You and Everett Bruce," Jillian said. "The two of you have been spotted all over the island from what I heard tonight. Unbelievable." She waved her arms in the air, making her point. "Cora Braddock and Sabrina Hodgson saw the two of you in Edgartown. More than once."

Angel took a deep breath, bit her bottom lip. She had hoped it would never come to this, foolishly perhaps. She and Everett had not exactly been discreet. She knew he could be recognized but had hoped that no one would recognize *her*.

"Well?" Jillian asked, the venom seeming to sprout from her gaze. "What do you have to say for yourself?"

Angel realized that there was no point in lying or being evasive at this point. She felt kind of relieved that the truth was out, actually. "Yes. It's true."

Jillian frowned, arched her back. "How the hell did this happen? How do you even know him? I mean, aside from when he was here as my guest. You two barely spoke."

Angel nodded. "I know . . ."

"And you never said a word to me," Jillian said, interrupting. "Not one word. Why not?"

Angel squared her shoulders and patiently held her tongue

as Jillian glared and tapped her foot, fuming. Any inclination Angel had felt to share information about her time with Everett was quickly vanishing under her employer's harsh gaze. She had expected some resistance but not this lashing out. She and Jillian weren't friends or confidants. Theirs was strictly a boss-employee relationship. She had no obligation to share anything about her personal life. Angel was trying to think of a gentle way to tell her this when Jillian suddenly removed a tissue from the pocket of her dress and dabbed the corners of her eyes.

"Seems I'm the last person on the entire island to know about this," Jillian said. "Even though you work for me. It's humiliating. Can't you see that?"

Angel's mouth dropped open with surprise. She had never seen Jillian get so worked up. But she supposed she could see how this could have been embarrassing for her. "I probably should have said something but I . . ."

"Yes, you should have," Jillian snapped. "And his dear wife barely buried after a tragic accident." She sniffed.

Any empathy Angel had felt a second ago faded as quickly as Jillian's tears. And there were those word again, *tragic accident.* "What happened to her?" Angel asked. "His wife?"

Jillian, eyes wide, stared at her. "You mean he hasn't told you?"

Angel shook her head. "No," she said softly. It seemed too difficult for him to discuss, and she had decided not to push, to simply enjoy these days with him.

Jillian scoffed. "Then I'm not going to tell you. The two of you are so close, let him do that. She's probably turning in her grave at the thought of her husband spending so much time with . . ." Jillian paused for dramatic effect and looked Angel up and down. "With a cook."

Angel shifted from one foot to the other. Her jaw tightened. That was rude, even for Jillian Harrison. There was no need to refer to her line of work in that derisive tone. None whatsoever.

And she was tempted to remind Jillian that it had been a year since his wife's death. Or that she had wanted to introduce him to Norma. It hadn't seemed too soon for that.

"We . . . we're just friends," Angel said. It dawned on her that putting Jillian at ease was more important than correcting her misstatements if she wanted to have even a faint chance of getting the evening off tomorrow. Mrs. Harrison would now suspect that any request for time off would be to spend time with Everett.

"I should certainly hope so," Jillian said. "Even that I don't understand. At all. You two haven't a single thing in common."

How wrong she was about that, Angel thought. She and Everett had a lot in common. But Jillian would never understand, even if she tried to explain until the sun came up.

"And you're nothing like his wife," Jillian continued. "She had so much class and was one of the most gorgeous women I've ever met."

Ouch! That was like a dagger in the back.

"Go on," Jillian said, dismissing Angel with a wave of her hand.

Angel slipped back up the stairs silently, sorrowfully, ever mindful that the prospect of getting away the following evening looked grim now, the odds slim to none.

* * *

Angel spent a fitful night tossing around in bed, unsure of how to deal with all that had transpired with Jillian. They had never gotten into such a heated dispute before, and it sickened Angel to her stomach that she'd let Jillian speak to her that way. There were moments she thought of just quitting and going back home to her regular job at the restaurant. She didn't need all this aggravation. That was if Jillian didn't fire her first.

She got up early the following morning, determined to try

and make the trip to Menemsha with Everett. She felt she deserved it, had every right to a fun evening with him, despite Jillian's hurtful words and obvious disapproval.

As usual, as she tidied up the kitchen after breakfast, Irvin grabbed his rackets and dashed off to play tennis with his buddies. Norma, carrying a small pile of books, slipped out to walk down to Inkwell Beach. It was a spectacular day, perfect for watching the sun drop down over the horizon at Menemsha. As soon as Angel finished stacking the dishwasher, she walked all around the lower level of the house, from one room to the next, searching for Jillian. Unable to locate her in all the expected places—her sitting room or on one of the screened porches—Angel climbed the stairs to the bedroom suites. She had no idea how Jillian and Irvin slept at home in DC, but here they had separate primary bedrooms. Jillian's was at the front of the house, with a massive balcony overlooking the ocean. Irvin's faced Ocean Park, an expansive grassy area with a large gazebo and walking paths leading in various directions.

The door was open; Angel could see Jillian sitting on her couch on the balcony while chatting on the phone. She backed away and waited, then returned a few minutes later, just as Jillian entered the bedroom.

"Mrs. Harrison, may I speak to you for a moment?"

Jillian paused on the opposite side of the room. Judging from the cool expression on her face, Angel was sure that their exchange the night before was still fresh on her mind. "Yes, Angel, what is it?"

She hesitated for a few seconds to gather her thoughts, even though she'd gone over what she would say countless times, all morning long. Could she lose her job by bringing this up? Maybe. The bitterness in Jillian's voice from last night had turned to an icy chill. Not a great start. But Angel didn't want to think that far ahead for now.

"I was hoping to get some time off later today." Might as well get right to it, Angel had decided. "I'll fix some lasagna and a salad and leave it in the fridge for you all to heat up when you're ready. I wanted to leave here around four or . . ."

"And your plans are . . . ?"

Angel cleared her throat, resisting the temptation to tell her boss it was none of her business. But that would only make things worse. "Driving out to Menemsha."

Jillian paused and looked down at her elegantly manicured fingernails. "How will you get there?"

Angel hesitated again.

"With Everett?" Jillian asked.

Angel nodded reluctantly. "Yes."

Jillian scoffed loudly.

"Like I said, I can fix everything before—"

"I'm afraid that will be impossible," Jillian said, interrupting. "We're having guests for dinner. I'll need you to fix something special and then clean up."

Angel eyes widened. What? Maybe she had misunderstood. "This is the first I've heard of that. You mean tonight?"

"That's what I just said. We're having one more gathering here before we leave. We can discuss the menu in about an hour, then you'll need to go to the market while I make some calls."

Angel felt her shoulders drop down to her knees. When had Jillian decided this? Just now? Did Irvin even know about it? Probably not. It was all Angel could do not to curse this woman out. To tell her to go straight to hell and then walk out of the house. For good. But the more she thought about it, the more she knew she would never do that. Her job, at least for now, was a sure thing for the future. Everett was not. She turned abruptly and fled from the room.

Everett sounded surprised when she called and told him everything—that Mrs. Harrison knew all about them, that she was having an impromptu dinner party, and that their drive down to Menemsha together that evening was off.

"Damn. Are you serious? Should I give her a call?" He seemed angry but like he was trying to hold it in. "Maybe I can reason with her. Just say the word."

Angel was torn. That might work but it could backfire terribly, especially since Mrs. Harrison now knew that they had been seeing each other surreptitiously. Jillian would never dare to utter a harsh word to Everett. *She* would be the one dealing with the consequences of her boss's wrath. She took a deep breath. "No, Everett. It's sweet of you to offer but I can't be sure that will help. It could even make things worse."

"Are you positive? I could at least give it a try."

The family was leaving on Saturday, the day after tomorrow, and that meant the same for her. Until then she would be under the watchful eye of Jillian and might not be able to slip away to see Everett again at all, at least not on the island. And who knew what would happen once they both got back to DC several weeks from now. He could—and probably would—forget all about her. This entire episode, from Jillian's cruel words to her total command over Angel's actions, had driven home the point that she was just a little old chef. A cook, as Mrs. Harrison had so clearly pointed out. She was not a classy lady like Everett's late wife and was undeserving of a man like Everett. Angel was disappointed and upset all at once. As much with herself for being stuck in this position as with Jillian. She could barely get the words out of her mouth.

"Yes, I'm positive."

6

The following afternoon, Angel perched on top of her stuffed suitcase. She bounced up and down, struggling mightily to close it, same as she had all the summers since becoming a personal chef for the Harrisons. Except this had been no ordinary summer. Far from it. Leaving the island was always a bit of a mixed bag for her emotionally, a bitter reminder of the fast-approaching end of lazy summer days and the cold, wintry weeks ahead. Yet it also felt satisfying to head back to the familiarity of her job and friends at home. And she always looked forward to having more time to work on recipes for her soups and salads cookbook.

Still, this time the sadness was hitting so much harder, with a sharp ache piercing the pit of her stomach. She was going to miss the jaunts all around Martha's Vineyard with Everett in his swanky silver convertible, laughing and teasing each other like old friends. And the cozy way he made her feel when he glanced over and smiled at her while driving, as she relayed tales of her early days visiting the island as a kid—about the shopping trips with her mom on Circuit Avenue and how her dad had taught her to swim at Inkwell Beach.

She sighed now as she stood and stared at the suitcase on her bed, finally zipped shut, her mind wandering elsewhere. It was odd how much Everett had grown on her so quickly. A mere couple of weeks had flown by. She thought about him constantly when they weren't together. But she had to stop that. They were over, done. If they'd ever even started. She hardly thought about Gene anymore. And when she did, she knew exactly what she had to do when she got back home. Break up with him. But instead of dreading the prospect, she now looked forward to it. If nothing else, her time with Everett had convinced her that she deserved better. Much better.

A soft tap at the door snatched her from her daydreams. As soon as she said, "Come in," it swung wide open. She was surprised to see Norma enter the room—her wire-framed glasses sitting at the edge of her nose—as she rarely did so. Angel was even more surprised by the obvious expression of concern on Norma's face.

"It's Mama," she said, breathlessly. "She's not feeling well. She was up all night coughing. Now she has a terrible headache and a fever."

Angel frowned. "I noticed she wasn't at breakfast this morning. What's wrong? It's not Covid, is it?"

Norma shook her head. "The doctor just left. It's some kind of respiratory virus with a long name I can't remember but not Covid. He says she won't be able to travel for at least two more weeks."

Irvin appeared in the doorway, a half-full glass of red wine in his hand. "Mind if I come in?" he asked while squeezing into the tiny bedroom, not much larger than a fair-size walk-in closet. The three of them stood awkwardly facing one another in the narrow space between the only two pieces of furniture in the room, a dresser and a double bed. Norma, with her arms folded across her white cotton blouse; Irvin, with his spare hand shoved into the pocket of his cargo shorts.

"I'm sorry to hear about Mrs. Harrison," Angel said. "Is there anything I can do?"

"As a matter of fact, yes," Irvin said. "This came on so suddenly, and Norma and I really must get back to DC for work. We head out first thing in the morning."

A sneaking suspicion of what was about to come crept up Angel's spine. She braced herself.

"Do you think you could stay a couple more weeks?" Norma asked.

"You mean with your mom?" Angel asked. "Just me?" Even though she'd expected it, it still took her by surprise. This was a family affair. A medical affair. She wasn't family. And she had no medical experience whatsoever.

Norma and Irvin both nodded.

Angel shook her head slowly at first, then more firmly. She felt a little uncomfortable saying no to her employer. But no, nope, no way. This was neither her job nor her problem. As much as she craved more time with Everett, the stark reality that there could never be anything lasting between the two of them was beginning to really sink in. And she definitely did *not* want to be stuck there alone with Jillian Harrison after that tension yesterday. She took a deep breath. "Ah, I have to get back to work on Monday myself. Sorry."

"I've already called and explained the situation to your employer," Irvin said. "They weren't happy about it but agreed to give you more time off."

Angel's jaw dropped. "You called my boss at Georgia's? Without even asking me first?" How presumptuous. Unbelievable. She shook her head again. "I could not possibly stay," she said. "I have so many other things I need to get . . ."

"We would double your usual weekly pay and add a thousand-dollar bonus," Irvin added.

Angel blinked. Had she heard that right? "Really?" That was a lot of money. The extra dollars could go a long way toward self-publishing and marketing her cookbook if she couldn't land a publisher. So far, she was not having any luck with agents.

"All you have to do is prepare a couple of light meals a day for her," Norma added. "I seriously doubt she'll want to eat much more than that."

"I agree," Irvin said. "Look, I know she's not the easiest person to deal with at times, but she'll be confined to her bed most—"

"Daddy!" Norma said.

"What?" Irvin said. "It's true. You and I both know it, Norma."

"Still, I don't think you should say stuff like that around . . ." Norma's head gestured slightly toward Angel.

Irvin shrugged. "It's no secret that . . ."

Angel cleared her throat, shifted uncomfortably from one flip-flop to the other. She could barely believe they were arguing about Jillian in front of her while the three of them were packed inside this tiny room on a ninety-degree day. The space was beginning to feel more than a little stuffy. "Okay. I'll stay."

"Oh? Perfect," Norma said.

"Excellent," Irvin said. "Now you want to be careful to protect yourself. We set up a table just inside her doorway. You can leave the meals there. That's it. Other than that, you're free. Any problems, just call me, but I really doubt you'll have any trouble. She's feeling pretty miserable and . . ."

As Angel listened to Irvin's instructions, her thoughts drifted. It sounded like he had been confident she would agree to stay if he teased enough cash her way. Was she being taken for granted? Had she agreed to stick around for two more weeks too readily, even given all the extra pay? What if she came to regret her decision? Highly possible. She exhaled, tried to push the negative thoughts aside. How much trouble could Jillian be while laid up sick in bed? Angel figured she was about to find out.

That evening while preparing dinner, she debated whether to call Everett and fill him in on the latest development. That internal debate lasted for a few hot minutes. There was no question she would call him as soon as she was done. She was so excited about spending more time with him in the days ahead that she cleared the kitchen in record time. On the way up to her room, she stopped and knocked gently on Jillian's door. "Yes," came a voice so weak and hoarse that Angel barely recognized it. She opened the door slowly and placed a tray on the table just inside. "I brought you some soup and a salad," she said softly.

Without glancing up from the covers, Jillian lifted an arm and waved Angel off, then reached for a couple of tissues from the box on her nightstand. She was blowing her nose loudly as Angel quietly shut the door.

No sooner had Angel entered her bedroom than her cell phone buzzed. She picked it up to see a text from Everett asking her to call when she got a moment so they could chat before she left in the morning. She sat on the bed, crossed her legs, and dialed his number, eager to share the news with him.

As soon as they hung up, she dialed another number.

"Hello. Gene?"

"Oh, hey," he said.

"Who is that?" came a soft voice Angel was unfamiliar with. A woman's voice.

"Uh, give me a second," Gene said. Angel could hear a lot of rustling on the line, then things went quiet. She tapped her foot with impatience while waiting for her soon-to-be ex-boyfriend to get himself together.

"Hey, baby, what's up?" he said, a little breathlessly. Angel could tell he had moved to another location. Probably the next room, sans whatever woman was there with him.

"Not going to talk long, just wanted to tell you something."

"Yeah?"

"It's over. We're done."

* * *

The next two weeks were a whirl of activity, leaving Angel giddy with happiness. She would leave breakfast for Jillian in the mornings, then rush out to hop into Everett's waiting Maserati. She'd return in the early evenings to prepare and leave a light dinner for Jillian, usually soup or a stew of some kind, and most nights dash right back out to meet up with him for dinner or drinks. They hit the seafood markets in Menemsha, the air filled with the scent of freshly caught fish and crustaceans, then sat on the small, rocky shore and munched on clam chowder. They cheered with the crowd as the cherry red sun dipped below the horizon. A couple of mornings she was able to get out early and join him for the hour-long wait for breakfast at the ever-popular ArtCliff Diner. She was loving every moment of her extended stay, could hardly believe he was still devoting so much of his free time to little old her. There were fleeting seconds when she wondered why he didn't spend more time with wealthy friends or business acquaintances, but she didn't allow herself to dwell on those thoughts for long.

One evening he surprised her and had a chef prepare and serve a fabulous seafood dinner for them on one of the decks at the house where he'd been staying while the owners—a plastic surgeon and his corporate-attorney wife—were out of the country. Or more aptly, the waterfront estate where he was staying; the massive dwelling stood on several sprawling acres of lush greenery facing the Edgartown Great Pond. She had pulled her wavy reddish-brown hair up into an artsy bun and wore a black low-cut dress, one of the two dressy outfits she'd brought with her to the island. She even added a silvery choker to highlight her long, slender neck.

That was the night they finally shared their first kiss, while standing on the deck under the moonlight. They had been slow dancing to the romantic music in their heads as the sweet earthy aroma of mint and other herbs drifted up from a garden nearby when he leaned in and brushed her lips with his. Then he kissed her again, a passionate moment that she wanted never to end.

It was also the night of their first argument.

They'd just reentered the house after the meal and unforgettable kisses when Everett excused himself to grab two glasses of wine, leaving her in a vast, great room admiring some of the incredible artwork that was on display throughout the house. Elaborately framed pieces adorned just about every wall, including what she suspected was an original abstract by Jackson Pollock hanging above an enormous marble fireplace. It nearly took her breath away when she realized exactly what she was gazing at. This was her first time seeing a painting by such a renowned artist in a private collection; she stood to study it more closely, her eyes scanning every inch of the masterpiece.

She was about to sit back down in a stuffed armchair when she heard Everett chatting on the phone in a room nearby and decided to wander a bit while waiting for him. She soon found herself in what appeared to be a large den full of rich-looking wood furniture and leather-bound books. She got excited, hoping to discover rare editions of classics but what she found instead, judging from a few titles, were thick law and medical books. Okay, boring, she thought as she backed away to exit the room.

Just as she approached the doorway, she noticed a small stack of leather binders and non-legal-looking books sitting on an end table near the couch. She walked over and glanced down, quickly realizing that they were related to finance. The exception was a book of poetry by Amanda Gorman that she had heard about but had not read. When she lifted it, a single sheet of ivory-colored stationary fluttered onto the floor. She retrieved the handwritten note and read it—

> My darling Everett,
>   Happy third anniversary.
>
>   Your loving wife,
>   C—

Angel was startled to realize what she was holding in her hand. A personal note from Chloe to Everett. In a way it felt like she was intruding. She was about to slip it back into the book but didn't have time, as a deep, sharp voice from behind pierced the room.

"What are you doing in here?"

She turned to see Everett staring at her from the doorway, holding two glasses of wine. He did not look pleased.

She froze, the book in one hand, note in the other. "I . . . I was just . . ."

He placed the glasses on the desk, marched across the room, and glanced down at the end table, where she'd obviously disturbed things. He snatched first the note, then the book from her hands.

"You shouldn't be in here, Angel. And you certainly should not be snooping around in my papers. What the hell do you think you're doing?"

She was astonished by his reaction. Or overreaction, really. Why was he suddenly so tense? So edgy? "It's just a book of poems and a note from your late wife. What's the big deal? You act like I just discovered something horrible about you and her."

He grimaced, clenched his jaw. She immediately regretted her words.

"I'm sorry," she said. "I should never have said that."

"You remind me of her at times."

She blinked. "What do you mean?"

"The flippant remarks. The casual attitude about important things or life in general. She did that a lot. Could get so annoying."

"I see," Angel said, swallowing hard. "I should not have brushed it off like that. I understand her death is still raw."

He shook his head. "It isn't even about that. Or her. Those folders are related to my work. They contain sensitive information about my business clients. They're for my eyes only."

"Oh. Okay. I get it. I didn't even open them, if that makes you feel better."

"What are you doing in this room anyway?" he asked, still seeming tight. "This is their personal library. It's not really intended for guests."

Now she was starting to feel guilty. "I was admiring the artwork while you were on the phone and I wandered in here when I saw all the books and . . ." She paused, feeling increasingly uneasy about the way this was going. He was different. Questioning her. Accusing her. She had meant no harm. "You know what? I should get going. Thank you for a lovely meal."

He frowned. "Hold on. You're leaving?"

"Yes, that's probably best." She walked out the library door.

"But we're miles away from your house," he protested. "How will you get back?"

"Easy. I'll call a cab," she said, walking briskly across the carpeted hallway. He was trying to make her feel ashamed when she really had done nothing wrong. And she didn't like it. Not one bit. Even though taxi service could be slow on the island, she needed to get away from this man.

He walked closely behind as she strode into the sitting room and snatched her purse from a stuffed chair.

"If you insist on leaving now, at least let me take you," he said.

"There's no need." She hastily dialed a number. With no car of her own on the island, she had long since become familiar with the cab services available.

"Then I insist on calling a private car for you."

She held up a hand as if to block the sound of his voice. "No. I can take care of myself."

"Of course you can take care of yourself," he said exasperatedly as he followed her toward the front door. "That's not the point."

Ignoring him, she let herself out to the spacious columned veranda to wait. It was hot and muggy, typical for August, but preferable to being inside with him. She noticed him peering out of a window, watching her, and deliberately turned her back. Twice he opened the door and asked if she was sure she didn't want him to drive her. Both times she shook her head firmly and remained silent.

All through the ride home, she found her mind turning to dark corners in her thoughts about him. She kind of understood the reluctance to talk about his late wife. She'd died violently not that long ago. But why was he so sensitive and guarded about his work? Could he be hiding something? A lot of successful businessmen did things that were unethical or even illegal, like evading taxes or stealing from their clients. She had barely touched those binders before he laid into her. All this secretive behavior was beginning to get to her. She realized she might be going way overboard with this thinking, but she'd become attached to the man and wanted to be careful before she got in any deeper. She couldn't wait to get home to her laptop to check him out.

As soon as the cab dropped her in front of the house, she

walked up to Jillian's bedroom and cracked the door open, hoping to see her boss resting peacefully.

But Jillian lifted her head. "Angel, is that you?"

Angel forced a smile. "Yes, Mrs. Harrison."

"Goodness. About time you got back," Jillian said weakly between coughs.

"Can I get you something?" Angel asked, fervently hoping the response would be no so that she could get to her room and her laptop.

"Maybe some tea with lemon. No. Make it ginger tea."

Angel raced down to the kitchen and popped a mug full of water into the microwave. She peeled the ginger while waiting, thinking of terms she could use to search for details about Everett's business dealings. *Investor, businessman, investment funds.* It felt like she was sneaking behind his back, but he left her little choice. Several minutes later she was placing a steaming mug on the tray in Jillian's room. "Anything else?" she asked, only to hear Jillian snore in return.

She hurried to her bedroom, sat on the edge of her bed, and opened her laptop.

Everett Bruce, Potomac, Maryland. She was about to enter more terms but there was no need to bother. Dozens of URLs instantly popped up about his private equity firm, Bruce Inc., headquartered in Washington, DC. He had founded the firm about ten years earlier and already had a staff of more than one hundred employees and billions of dollars in assets, invested mainly in technology. All the articles she found were glowing with positive reviews of him, his business, and his many philanthropic activities in education and health care.

She had known Everett Bruce was a big deal, especially as a Black man, but until now she'd had no real sense of just how big he was. As she skimmed through the web pages—including a list of some of the prestigious companies he'd invested in and acquired—she began to sense why he was so sensitive about his business paperwork. He had a lot of very important and high-profile partners and clients.

An hour later, she closed the browser window in complete awe. It was amazing that this powerful and revered businessman seemed so regular, so down-to-earth. And mind-boggling to think that he had wanted to spend his precious time with her. She wondered now, as she thought back to her behavior during their last moments at the house, if perhaps her own insecurities about her worthiness of a relationship with him had gotten the better of her. She closed her computer, sighed heavily, and stretched across the bed, hoping she hadn't completely blown things with him.

7

A couple of days later, Angel was still agonizing over Everett Bruce as she walked down the stairs to start working. She hadn't heard from him since that fateful evening at the house, when their relationship had seemed to turn upside down out of the blue, and she wasn't sure what to make of that. Twice she had reached for her phone and started to dial his number only to back down, unsure whether she was ready to face what he might have to say.

To her surprise, she found Jillian in the kitchen, dressed in a flowy caftan, opening one upper cabinet after another. Angel hadn't expected her to be up and about just yet and had taken to sleeping in thirty or so minutes later than usual. They were only ten days into what Angel had assumed would be at least two weeks of bed rest. But here Jillian was, flitting about, as if desperately searching for something.

"Good morning, Mrs. Harrison. You're looking better. Can I get you anything?"

"Oh, there you are," Jillian said. "Where in the world do you keep the coffee pods? I've looked everywhere."

Angel walked to the cabinet just above the coffee machine. "Right up here. But you have a seat. I'll fix it for you."

Jillian collapsed breathlessly into a chair at the kitchen table. It was obvious that she should still be resting. "Why don't you go on back up, Mrs. Harrison? I'll bring the coffee to you in just a few minutes."

Jillian nodded, then slowly stood, steadying herself on the edge of the table. "I thought I was ready for this," she said between mild coughs. "I swear I'm going out of my mind cooped up in that room all day long."

"I get it," Angel said, spreading a white cloth napkin across a tray. "But you shouldn't rush things. Doctor's orders."

"Yes, and no doubt you would prefer I stay confined up there."

Angel paused, glanced up. "Why would you say that?"

"So you can continue, you know, running all about town." Jillian waved her arm for emphasis.

Angel remained silent, resumed setting up the tray. They would be in this house together for at least a few more days. She wanted to stay far, far away from this topic, if possible, and was determined not to take her employer's bait.

"Are you still spending much time with Everett?" Jillian asked, point-blank.

Angel exhaled as she considered the best way to respond. Normally he would have texted by now, suggesting some activity or another for them. She was trying her best not to dwell too much on what his silence might mean; it scared her to think she might have ruined their relationship by crossing a line. She preferred instead to believe that he just needed more time. After all, they had seen each other nearly every day for the past few weeks. They probably both needed some breathing room.

"Um, no, I'm not," Angel said. At least that was the truth for now.

"Really?" Jillian asked, her voice filled with doubt. "Someone said they saw you two a few nights ago on the beach in Menemsha."

Of course, Angel thought wryly, as she reached for one of Jillian's favorite coffee cups and a matching saucer. Jillian's island sleuths were hard at work everywhere, even while she lay sick in bed. "Well, yes, but I doubt I'll be seeing him again anytime soon."

"Did he hurt you, dear? I mean your feelings."

Angel stopped abruptly, unsure what to make of Jillian's words. She looked directly at her. "I'm fine."

"Mm-hmm. It's for the best, you know. Much better that whatever you two had going end sooner rather than later. Less painful. For you. Since nothing much could ever have come of it anyway."

Angel cringed, now perfectly aware of what Jillian was implying. That Everett was out of her league. That she was in way over her head, had been presumptuous to imagine he'd ever take her seriously. It hurt to even think these thoughts, but Angel had to admit she'd found herself toying with the very same ideas herself. She exhaled loudly and went back to the tray as Jillian inched toward the stairs. Still, it hit a little differently to hear someone else—especially Jillian—give a voice to her deepest, most anxious fears about Everett.

One thing Angel was certain of: she was not ready to confide in Mrs. Harrison. Would likely never be. Her boss was the last person she would ever reveal her feelings about Everett to. Or anything else, for that matter. "I'll bring this up in a minute."

"Some buttered cinnamon toast would be nice," Jillian said just before disappearing up the stairs.

"Of course," Angel muttered under her breath as she reached for the bread drawer.

Minutes later, she carried the tray upstairs. Then she decided that after that irritating discussion with her boss, the best way to soothe her soul would be to take some time to clear her head by doing the things she loved best. First, she whipped up a big breakfast of turkey bacon and an omelette for herself and ate it on the patio. A couple of hours later, she donned her floppy straw hat and strolled down to Inkwell Beach, sketch pad in hand. The huge crowd that descended on the island in August had thinned out now that it was early September. She looked forward to spending a quiet, relaxing day at the beach. Anything to take her mind off the events of the past few days.

She leaned back on her elbows and stared out at the ocean, watching the waves drift in and out as she wiggled her bare toes in the warm sand. Her sketch pad and pencils rested beside her on the beach blanket. She tried hard to focus on the rhythmic beat of the water dancing to and fro, rippling along the shore.

But it was hopeless. Jillian's harsh comments kept intruding on her thoughts.

Nothing much could ever have come of it.

Less painful. For you.

Angel wanted to scream over the roar of the ocean. She wanted to declare those words and their ugly implications utter nonsense. If her time with Everett had showed her anything, it was that he was not the kind of man Jillian and many others assumed. Not the kind of man who would have nothing to do with a woman like her. He was kind, thoughtful, considerate. He didn't care about her background or her past, only about what he saw and felt around her now.

That was what she wanted to shout out. What she wanted to believe. So badly. But was it actually true? Was it realistic? Was she naively fooling herself? She knew what the deal usually was. Men like Everett went for glamorous, stylish, polished women they could show off to their monied friends. The trophy wife. Women like Chloe. Angel would pit her natural looks against them any day. But she had no high-end designer clothes, no glam squad on call, no jewelry boxes full of rare diamonds and pearls. Or any of the other accoutrements of wealthy women who men like Everett were used to. For her it was usually plain old flip-flops and cutoff jeans, like what she had on now. Or simple sundresses. Had she been fooling herself to even hope that Everett could really be into her?

She sat up, grabbed her pad, and furiously tried to distract herself by sketching the sailboat out in the distance, the children building sandcastles on the shore. But it was hard to ignore the empty feeling in the pit of her stomach. And the nagging loneliness in her heart. It was going to take some time to move on. To get used to being on the island without him. She removed her hat and placed it over her eyes as she stretched out on the blanket. It wasn't long before she felt herself drifting in and out. She'd slept so little the previous two nights, tossing and turning, worrying herself ragged.

"So, there you are."

Her heart fluttered. Was that really Everett's voice? Or was she dreaming? She lifted the hat and squinted against the sun to see him standing above, smiling down at her. She watched in silence as he sat on the blanket beside her and picked up the sketch pad. "Nice," he said, flipping through the pages. "These are good."

She nodded in silence and sat up, trying to calm her emotions and gather her thoughts before she spoke.

"How are you?" he asked.

Truthfully? No, he didn't need to hear the truth. "I'm doing okay. How did you know I was here?"

"Lucky guess. I've been calling and texting you for over an hour."

Really? Angel grabbed her cotton beach bag and searched for her phone. That was when she realized she had left it behind while hurriedly gathering her blanket, towel, and pencils to escape the house and Jillian's scorching words.

"I must have left my phone at the house." Thank goodness it had a code and locked soon after she stopped using it.

He nodded and brushed sand from his hands. She was instantly reminded that the beach was not his thing. They sat quietly for a moment, their shoulders lightly touching, taking in the sun and sea. He reached for her hand, cupping it in his, and a sharp chill raced up her spine. It was all she could do not to pop up and break into a happy dance. But she kept her cool, waited for him to speak.

"It's beautiful out here," he said finally. "Despite all this sand."

She laughed. "What's so horrible about sand?"

"It gets everywhere. Into everything. That's why I don't get down to the ocean often. Unless it's on a boat."

"You said you came to the island once before. How long ago was that?"

He looked directly at her. "Yes, when I was first married. I'll tell you more about that if you have dinner with me tomorrow night."

She looked back at him and smiled. "I'd love to."

"Good. I was worried you didn't want to see me again after you stormed off the other day."

"Sorry about that."

"No need to apologize. I admire you for being curious and speaking your mind. I could have been more patient."

"Thank you. You said I remind you of her. How?"

He nodded and squeezed her hand. "Let's talk about that over dinner tomorrow. That okay with you? I'll make reservations at the Red Cat Kitchen for eight."

"That sounds good."

He walked her back to the house, then rounded the corner to his car. She was excited about having dinner for the first time at the Red Cat Kitchen. The garden-patio restaurant was known for its quirky atmosphere and delicious farm- and seafood-to-table dining, not to mention it was one of the places on the island where the Obamas had been spotted dining.

* * *

Jillian was up and about the following afternoon but said she'd have a light dinner in her bedroom that evening while watching movies on Netflix. Angel was so relieved. Although she had decided to tell Jillian the truth about dining with Everett if needed to get out of the house, she was thankful to be able to quietly slip away and around the corner into his waiting car at seven thirty.

They chatted nonstop all the way to the restaurant and were still talking as they started in on appetizers and drinks.

"So, tell me more about how I remind you of your late wife," she said during a brief lull in the conversation. She had been dying to get to this.

"She was a photographer when we met and was curious like you, in a different sort of way. I found it refreshing. At least at first."

Darn. She'd hoped he was going to say something about her also being "almost too beautiful."

As if he sensed her thoughts, he added: "And for the record, I find you just as attractive if not more. Unlike Chloe, I don't think you have any idea just how pretty you are. That's endearing."

She smiled and glanced downward. Though flattered, now she felt shy. "Thank you."

"It's true."

"What did you mean when you said you found her curiosity refreshing at first?"

"She was always wanting to try new things, like jumping out of planes or scuba diving or traveling to some exotic location halfway around the world. That's fine now and then, but it was never enough for her. It never ended. After one adventure she was immediately ready for the next. The first few years of our marriage we were constantly on the go—always traveling, entertaining. We spent a lot of time in Malibu and Hawaii. You name it."

"She had family on the West Coast?"

"No, we . . . I have homes there."

"Oh. Well, that all sounds exciting, actually."

"Like I said, it was at first but eventually it got tiring. At least for me. I wanted to slow things down after a while. To think about settling down and starting a family, having children. But she had other ideas. Didn't think she had the time or temperament for children. Chloe could be incredibly self-centered. The last six months or so of our marriage were miserable. By the time she died, we had drifted fairly far apart."

Angel nodded. So, he had wanted children and she hadn't. Interesting. "That sounds like it must have been incredibly difficult for you."

"It was."

She sighed. "I'm sorry you had to go through that, but I hope you don't think I'm self-centered."

"Oh no. That's where the two of you seem very different. Fortunately."

"Thank you."

He touched her hand gently as the waiter approached their table with the main courses.

"What happened to her?" Angel asked after he left.

"You mean, how did she die?"

"Do you mind me asking?"

"Not at all. It's no secret. It was reported briefly in the news at the time. It's just painful to talk about."

She nodded with empathy and waited while he fingered his wineglass. He inhaled deeply.

"She shot herself."

Angel caught her breath, covered her mouth. "Oh no."

His lips tightened.

"Oh my God." She slumped back in her seat, numb with disbelief.

8

Angel's jaw dropped; her gaze drifted away. Had Everett really just said what she thought he'd said? That his late wife had taken her own life? Angel said nothing. Her tongue was twisted into a knot.

"Now maybe you can understand why I'm so reluctant to talk about it," he added. "It was a horrible night."

"I get it." She had found her voice but somehow it didn't feel normal to her. It felt weak, scratchy. "That *is* horrible. But why? Why did she take her life? She had so much going for her."

"That I will never truly understand. She had a history of mild depression, on and off, and had threatened to take her life once. But I never took that seriously. I never expected her to actually do it." He took a generous gulp of wine, let out a deep gust of air. "We argued that night. I hated arguing with her. She would get to yelling and cursing, so I left the room. Walked over to Ida's place to get away for a minute. We heard a gunshot and rushed up to the bedroom. Found her lying on the floor, gun next to her."

He looked down at his plate. His face was pasty, shrunken; his eyes glazed over. She had never seen this confident, powerful man look so crestfallen. This was obviously still very hard on him. It could take him a long time to really get past this.

"That must have been awful for you."

"I still can't believe it happened." He paused, glanced away. "I don't even remember what we were arguing about. I left the room and then . . ."

"Jeez," Angel said. He was shaking now; her heart went out to him as she thought about what a frightful night it must have been. She reached out, took his hand into hers. "I'm glad Ida was with you. And you didn't have to go through that alone."

"It was a crazy night. Ambulances, the police everywhere." He inhaled deeply. "She was only thirty-nine. Too young to die."

Too young to die. Angel repeated the words in her head and squeezed his hand to comfort him. "Way too young." A dozen more questions swarmed through her mind. Like why had Chloe kept a gun if she'd had a history of depression? Did he know she had it? But all that would have to wait. She could see that he was still in a bad place. "How are you holding up?"

"Some days are easier than others, I admit, but I'm a lot better now than I was when it happened a year ago."

"Good."

He tried to smile. "You've helped tremendously."

"I have?"

He nodded. "Our time here has done so much to take my mind off things."

She smiled. It made her feel good to think that she had helped somehow.

"What a way to ruin our dinner, huh?" he said.

"Nonsense. I'm glad you finally opened up to me about this." She honestly was. It was unsettling, nerve-racking, shocking. All that and more. But it was a huge part of his past and better that she knew than to be left in the dark, wondering.

They talked little during the ride back to the house, each

deep in their own thoughts. Instead of sleeping that night, Angel found herself tossing and turning frantically, her mind racing. About Chloe. About the argument. About the gun and the dreadful, fateful events of that night. She hated the very idea of guns, that a cold, hard piece of metal could end a life in a split second. She had never even seen one in the flesh except on law enforcement. And hoped she never would.

Angel was certain that knowing all this would likely change the dynamic of their relationship. How could it not? But hopefully in a good way. Now that he was beginning to share more with her, they might grow even closer.

She wondered how much Jillian and others knew about this. Jillian had mentioned that something terrible had happened the night Chloe died, but did she have any idea of the horrific details?

* * *

"Such a shame all the way around," Jillian said the following afternoon as Angel served a lunch of crab soup and Caesar salad with mint juleps on a screened porch at the Harrison house. She had finally decided to fess up to Jillian, to be up front about dating Everett, including that they were back together. The relationship was getting more involved, not to mention more complicated. It was too tiresome trying to bother with hiding it from her boss. And Angel really wanted to learn more about Chloe after the news of the previous day. Jillian was the best person, actually the only person, she knew to ask.

Besides, she was a grown-ass woman; she could date anyone she pleased. If Jillian had a problem with her seeing Everett and decided to let her go, then so be it. She still had her job back at home. She would truly miss her all-expenses-paid trips to the island every summer, but she would be just fine. Although Angel had a feeling that, at this moment at least, Jillian, still coughing and sniffling between sips of her afternoon cocktail, needed Angel's help around the house more than she needed this job.

She had just informed Jillian about the suicide.

"All sorts of rumors were flying about at the time," Jillian replied. "The early news reports just said the gun went off accidentally. I thought maybe she was cleaning it or handling it for some reason. Then I think I did read or hear at some point about her shooting herself. The whole story got more and more convoluted and finally just fizzled out." Jillian furrowed her brows. "I found it hard to believe she would do that. I mean, Chloe had everything—brains, beauty, *money*. Are you sure that's what he told you?"

"Um, no, actually." Of course she was certain that was what he'd said. He'd been very clear. But now Angel seriously regretted running her mouth to Jillian, who could start talking all over town and get everyone gossiping, something Everett likely would not appreciate. Nor would she. She suddenly felt a need to protect Everett and the information he'd shared with her. Odd that she should feel the need to protect such a powerful man. But Jillian and the others in her circle of friends did not know him like Angel did. They had not seen the pure agony on his face when he explained in painful detail what had happened on that fateful night.

Angel cleared her throat. She needed to steer the focus away from the shooting. "I probably misunderstood. Did you know her? Personally?"

"You mean Chloe? Not all that well. I chatted with her a few times at social events but I know others who knew her much better. She and Everett were very outgoing. They had lots of friends, were always entertaining. Their dinner parties and annual spring ball were legendary."

Angel nodded. Everett had mentioned that they'd done a lot of entertaining in the early years of their marriage. "He says he began to lose interest in all that eventually."

"Now that you mention it, I have heard that she started showing up at affairs without him. Or she came with his sister, Ida. But that's not so unusual. Marriages tend to have their ups and downs."

"Of course."

"As for her personally," Jillian continued, "she came from a very prominent, well-respected local family. Her father was a neurosurgeon and her mother, a principal at one of the private schools in DC. The wedding was a huge, lavish affair. Her parents spared no expense. Everett's background, I believe, is more humble. His father was a bookkeeper. But by the time he and Chloe met, he had made a huge fortune. They purchased a multimillion-dollar mansion on River Road in Potomac that they named Riverwild Estate as well as several other homes and a private jet. They were *the* couple in the area. He brought the money, she the pedigree, as everyone always said. Perfect couple."

"Mm-hmm." Angel wasn't so sure all that made for the perfect couple. She suspected that Everett had come around to similar thinking based on some of the things he'd shared with her. But she would keep those thoughts to herself. "Can I get you anything else, Mrs. Harrison?"

"This looks fine. She had an enviable sense of style, you know."

"Excuse me?" Angel was just about to step back into the house.

"Chloe. The things she did were often over-the-top but always very, very classy. Very elegant. She had such flair. She redecorated the mansion and their other homes on the West Coast using the finest materials imported from all over the world and furnished them with millions of dollars' worth of antiques and artwork. They were featured in *Architectural Digest*. It takes a certain kind of upbringing to know how to pull all that off."

Point taken. It was so obvious what Jillian was up to. Trying to make sure Angel knew her place, that she understood that her upbringing had been nothing like Chloe's. Angel was certainly aware that the lifestyle Everett currently led was miles apart from her own. But unlike Everett, who never dwelled on the differences, Jillian was deliberately driving the stake in, making sure it was all crystal clear. Now Angel found herself wondering if Everett had downplayed the opulence of his lifestyle to help her feel more at ease around him.

She noticed Jillian watching her closely and quickly tried to wipe what must have been a dazed expression off her face. "Well, I should get going," Angel said, deciding not to dignify her employer's withering words with a response. "I want to do some grocery shopping and make your dinner before my date with Everett tonight." She picked up the serving tray, turned abruptly, and walked toward the doorway.

"I do hope you know what you're doing, you know," Jillian said to Angel's back. "The two of you have nothing in common. Sure, you're young and perky and pretty, and he's attracted to that. Just know that as soon as you leave the island, this little fling will end. He'll go back to his normal plush life and you to your ordinary one. Are you prepared for that?"

Angel paused and stiffened as she debated what to say, if anything.

"'Cause it doesn't seem like it," Jillian continued. "We women are different. We become emotionally attached. Men not so much, and I really don't want to see you get hurt, Angel, despite what you might think."

As much as the words stung, Angel knew there was likely much truth to them. That after this idyllic summer vacation, she and Everett could very well go back to Maryland and get on with their lives separately. He to his mega mansion in Potomac, she to her little one-bedroom condo in Takoma Park. But one thing Jillian had said that she completely disagreed with was that this was simply some wild, fun fling. Angel felt confident that Everett had genuine feelings for her, that he was not being deceptive about that. And her feelings for him were certainly all too real and growing steadily.

Angel turned back toward Jillian. "I get what you're saying," she said. "I just don't agree with it. I've gotten to know him pretty well."

Jillian looked doubtful, as if she had been about to say more but decided against it when she saw the steely-eyed expression on Angel's face. "Suit yourself," Jillian said. "How much longer will he be here on the island?"

"About a week. Maybe a little more. Then he goes to Europe on business."

"I see. Just be careful."

As Angel walked back to the kitchen, she thought about Jillian's last words: *Be careful*. It was already too late for that. She had thrown caution to the wind the day she'd stepped into the man's silver convertible and they'd sped off down the road. Then when she had continued to see him, on one date after another. She'd realized from the beginning that any relationship between them would likely never go beyond the shores of Martha's Vineyard. That she was risking having her heart torn into a million tiny pieces as her feelings for him intensified. Now that they had only days remaining was not the time to exercise caution.

9

This was the fifth time she'd stayed out all night in just as many days, Angel thought as she stood beneath a glittering crystal chandelier, patting her face dry in a luxurious bathroom that was easily ten times the size of her bedroom at the Harrison house. She and Everett were getting closer every day. She smiled as her thoughts drifted back to the memorable evening they'd just spent with a dozen of his friends aboard a two-hundred-foot superyacht off the coast of Martha's Vineyard. Everett was doing nothing if not spoiling her. She had to constantly remind herself that all this high living could—and probably would—vanish from her life someday. But no need to dwell on that now, she thought as she strolled toward the door. She was going to enjoy every enchanting moment while she could.

"You said she doesn't even get up until almost noon," Everett said, struggling to sit up in bed as she entered the bedroom all dressed and ready to go back to the Harrisons' that morning.

"I know. But I have work to do around the house if I want to keep my job," she said, slipping into her sandals. "And I do want to keep my job. You don't have to get up, though. I'll call a cab."

"No way," he said just before dashing into the bathroom. "I'll be ready to take you back in ten."

* * *

The next morning, Angel heard Everett turning on the shower as she stirred awake. She had slept longer than intended and was stretching beside the bed when she heard a knock. She glanced toward the closed washroom door, thinking Everett would emerge and then she could go in and grab a quick shower. When he didn't, she reached for a bathrobe, then remembered she didn't have one here; all she brought on these nightly excursions was sleepwear, toiletries, and a change of undies.

"Yes?" she asked, tugging at the hemline of her thigh-length nightie.

A plump, cheerful woman with sandy-brown hair, dressed in a light-colored shift and sensible shoes, entered bearing a tray with orange juice and coffee. A single red rose sat in a sleek glass vase. "Good morning, ma'am. Mr. Bruce said it would be too early for a full breakfast for you. That you'd take juice and coffee only."

Angel nodded slowly. This felt so odd. She wasn't used to anyone waiting on *her*. "Um, yes, that sounds good. Thank you."

The servant carried the tray toward the bed and paused. "Would you like it here? Or would you prefer I place it there for you?" she asked, beckoning toward the small round table and two chairs across the room.

"Oh. I'll take it here." Angel scooted back in bed. "Thank you again," she said, before the woman exited and softly shut the door. She took a sip of what had to be the most delightful cup of coffee she'd ever tasted, all the while reminding herself that she needed to get up and get herself back to the Harrison house. Everett stepped out of the bathroom, a towel draped around his waist.

"You look happy," he said, smiling at her as he brushed his hair.

Her smile broadened at the sight of his figure standing in the doorway; he looked tall and handsome as ever. Looking at his bare chest, she was reminded that he worked out. His daily routine, whatever it involved, was doing a stellar job of keeping his forty-five-year-old physique in top shape. "Mmm," she murmured over her coffee cup.

"Do you want me to get Julia to bring you another?" he asked. Angel realized that he had assumed the sound coming from her throat referred to the brew and not his body. She decided to let it slide for now. Or she might never get back to the house.

"No, I'm good," she said. "But what kind of coffee is this? It's amazing."

He shrugged. "You'd have to ask the chef."

"Which reminds me," she said, hopping up with the tray. "I really do need to get going. Like now. She's getting up earlier and earlier lately, and it's already past seven." Normally Angel would be padding up the stairs of the Harrison household by 6:30 a.m. But watching the purples and oranges together again from the deck of the yacht as the sun set had led to one of their most romantic evenings ever. Their lovemaking had lingered long into the morning hours.

Before she could take another step, Everett gently removed the tray from her grasp. "Here, I'll take that." He placed it on the table, then playfully swooped her up midstride. She laughed.

"What's gotten into you?" she asked as he waltzed around the room with her in his arms. He dropped her onto the bed playfully and smiled as she bounced, his eyes filled with merriment.

"You're in a really upbeat mood this morning," she said between her own fits of giggles as he sat down beside her.

"If I am, it's all your doing," he said. "No one has ever lifted my spirits the way you always do. Being around you makes me happy." He leaned down and kissed her warmly. She rubbed his arm affectionately; she so enjoyed seeing him in high spirits, something she was witnessing much more often of late.

"Are you sure I can't convince you to hang around with me here a little longer?" he asked, his gaze slowly changing from one of merriment to open desire, his hand slipping beneath her nightie. She loved seeing this expression on his face and found it terribly hard to resist. She cupped his cheeks in her hands as he glided her down toward the bed.

"You're doing a good job of persuading me," she said teasingly.

When he kissed her again, this time more hungrily, she knew she was going to be awfully late getting back to work that morning.

* * *

It always felt foolish to quietly slip out of her sandals then tiptoe up the stairs and past Jillian's bedroom. But that had become her routine. Luckily Jillian was still fast asleep when Angel returned later than usual that morning, and she had no desire to awaken her boss. Partly out of kindness, but more for selfish reasons; a peacefully slumbering Jillian equaled a less bothersome Jillian. Although Angel was fairly certain that her employer had to be somewhat aware of these furtive nightly escapades, Jillian had decided, who knew why, not to bring them up. Regardless of the reason, Angel was thankful.

A couple of hours later, Everett parked around the corner from the house, and Angel slipped out after leaving breakfast just inside the doorway to Jillian's room. "Sorry you have to keep sneaking around like this," he said.

She laughed softly. "No, you aren't. And neither am I."

He chuckled. "You're right. But I hope you don't get into any trouble because of me."

"Don't worry. I'll deal with it."

"So, how much longer do you think you'll be here on the island?" he asked.

"It's hard to say. She's definitely doing much better, although she hasn't said anything about leaving yet. A few days at least, I'm guessing."

He reached over, took both her hands into his, and looked directly into her eyes. "I'm really going to miss you, my Angel."

She caught her breath. The moment between them was electric. Yet as much as his words were music to her ears, they also brought a sharp reality closer to home. Soon they would have to leave this paradise and part ways. "Me, too."

"I mean, really, really miss you. You have no idea how much."

She swallowed the lump in her throat. The thought of being apart filled her with anguish. Which was why she generally tried to avoid thinking about it.

He brought both her hands to his lips, kissed them softly. "I'll call you every day while I'm traveling until I get back to the States."

"That would be so nice." Though she was hopeful that he meant it when he said he'd keep in touch, deep down she knew it was unlikely he'd follow through on his promises. Maybe he would for a short while but long term, not much chance. He'd go back to his affluent, charmed lifestyle, flying all around in his private jet, conducting business, giving speeches, and settling back into his multimillion-dollar mansion in Potomac. In no time at all, he would forget all about Angel in her little condo in Takoma Park. They probably lived within twenty miles of each other, but they might as well be on opposite ends of the planet. Which was why these sweet moments when he vowed that their relationship would continue often brought her to the brink of tears instead of uplifting her.

"You don't sound convinced," he said.

"I would love nothing more than to continue seeing you, Everett. These weeks have been magical for me. But if we're honest . . ." She paused, not even wanting to voice the negative thoughts swimming around in her head, as if she could somehow prevent them from materializing by keeping them to herself.

"What? Go ahead. Say what it is you're thinking."

She exhaled. "Our lives couldn't be more different. You know that. Have you ever even dated a woman like me?"

He blinked. "What does *that* mean?"

"You know," she said, laughing awkwardly. "A regular woman with no money and no pedigree."

He thought for a moment. "Not since I was in my twenties or early thirties, but that's what I love about us. We're different. *You're* different. I admit this is sort of new for me but it's also very refreshing. And comforting. I can't really explain it but I feel so much more at ease with you than I have with any woman in years. Maybe ever. With Chloe, things were always so intense, you know. Do this, go there. Buy this, get that. The pressure and the expectations to always be on top, to 'maintain our status'"— he made little quotation marks with his fingers—"as she always said, were tiring. It consumed us. In a lot of ways, that lifestyle can be rigid and confining." He shook his head. "I honestly never want to go back to that. I like what we have. You and me. Do you believe that?"

She nodded. She certainly *wanted* to believe it.

"Good," he said. "Because it's the truth." He kissed her hands again. "I'm looking forward to dinner tonight."

"So am I." She had promised to cook for him, anything his heart desired, and was startled when he quickly asked for meat loaf, mashed potatoes, and kale greens cooked in the old-fashioned Southern style. Naturally, she'd been devising ways to elevate the meal, perhaps by adding ground veal and wine to the meat loaf. But now she realized that she shouldn't have been surprised by his simple request. He was really a country boy at heart, born and raised in rural Virginia. She was beginning to appreciate that deep at the core, beneath the polished, high-flying exterior, beneath the prestigious college degrees, Everett Bruce was a simple guy. It sometimes felt to her as if a part of this busy businessman desperately craved a humbler home life.

They kissed goodbye and she let herself into the foyer. As she slipped out of her sandals, Everett's last words about savoring their moments together played over and over in her head, soothing and comforting her spirits. She passed by Jillian's bedroom door, deep in thought. He had given her a much-needed glimmer of hope for their future together as a couple.

"Angel?"

She paused midstep, turned around. Jillian was standing in her doorway in a flowery pink-and-green dress with spaghetti straps. She had a big smile on her face as she dropped a long strand of pearls into a small silken tote bag. Behind her, on the floor of the bedroom, Angel glimpsed several packed suitcases. Another one, half-full, sat open on a luggage rack.

Angel took it all in with apprehension, her chest filling with dread at what she imagined was coming. "Yes, Mrs. Harrison?"

"I booked flights for us tomorrow morning. I've already started packing. We're finally going home. Isn't that wonderful? I am so sick and tired of these four walls, ready to get off this island. Three weeks is way too long for anyone to be ill and confined to any room."

Jillian stopped talking, obviously waiting for a response from Angel. But Angel was much too disheartened to speak. Too stunned and disappointed. This was her worst nightmare coming true. It felt as if she were being crushed, the world smashing down around her. She'd known this moment was getting closer by the day but still thought she had a little more time; Jillian had not said a word about leaving. Not a single word. How could she spring this on Angel with absolutely no notice? With all the late nights out, Jillian had to have known she was spending a lot of time with Everett and would have appreciated some type of heads-up. Some type of warning. But no, Jillian had decided to announce this out of the blue. Maybe even deliberately. Angel's pounding heart felt like it was about to burst out of her chest.

She had to get out of that hallway, away from Jillian, so she could think. So she could breathe. She didn't want her boss to see what she knew must be pure misery on her face. She glanced away. "Fine, Mrs. Harrison," she said quietly, her voice feeling uncontrollably weak.

Without another word, she turned on her heels and fled down the hallway to her bedroom. She sank down onto the bed, fell back, covered her face with her hands. Everett's smile flashed before her, and she blinked hard to try and hold back tears that suddenly flooded her eyes. But it was hopeless. They flowed freely down her cheeks.

She sat up abruptly. She needed to see Everett, to talk to him. Maybe he could find some way to make it all better. But the more she thought about the circumstances, the less she believed he could actually do that. They had known each other for such a short time. Would he even really want to? Jillian's packed luggage had felt like a heavy dose of reality smacking her upside her head.

She took a deep breath, wiped away the tears, then walked down the hallway to the bathroom and splashed water on her face. She patted herself dry and stared at her reflection in the mirror, willing herself to go through with what she knew had to be done. As much as she dreaded it, better to rip the Band-Aid off now, free and clear of any stupid hopes and dreams. This had been a wondrous summer, but now it was over.

Back in her bedroom, she reached for her cell phone and called Everett.

* * *

His reaction was swift and not exactly what she'd been expecting. She had somehow thought he would protest at first but eventually see that it made sense to say their goodbyes now.

"No," he said firmly, interrupting as she tried to explain why she thought it best they end things now without imposing any idle declarations or expectations about the future. "I'm coming to get you, Angel. We have to talk about this."

"I can't possibly leave here now, Everett. I have to prepare breakfast. Then I have to pack all my things and arrange for someone to pick me up at the airport in DC. I . . ."

"Angel, listen to me. We can't end it like this."

It was tempting to give in and see him again, even once more. So tempting. But she was convinced that prolonging this would only cause more pain for her in the long run. "I'm sorry, Everett. I have to do it this way. For myself. Please understand."

"No, I don't understand. I don't agree with this."

She shook her head silently to reinforce her conviction that she was doing the right thing.

"I'll call Jillian and speak to her about giving you some time to see me," he said. "I'll let her know . . ."

"No. Please don't do that," she said, interrupting. She paused, trying to gather her thoughts. He was obviously not going to be put off easily, and she would rather try to slip away for a few moments than have him say anything to Jillian. No telling how that would turn out. "Okay. I'll meet you."

"Excellent. When?"

"In an hour but only for a couple of minutes."

* * *

The second Angel slipped into the passenger seat of Everett's car, he pulled off.

"Where are you going?" she asked. "Why can't we talk here?"

"I'm only driving to a more secluded spot nearby." He patted her on the leg. "Relax. We won't be long."

She noted the look of steely determination on his face and decided to simply savor the moment. This would be the last time she'd sit next to him in his convertible with the top down, the cool ocean breeze whipping across their faces. Stop fighting it, she told herself. Stop fighting him.

He soon pulled into a space not far from the Oak Bluffs terminal and faced the ocean. They watched in silence as one of the ferries pulled slowly into the harbor. He seemed to be gathering his thoughts, as was she.

He turned to face her. "Tell me what happened when you got back this morning."

"Well," she replied, as the memory of seeing Jillian's luggage hit her, "just as I said. She's already packed and ready to go. She booked our flights for tomorrow morning at ten. That means I have to pack tonight. And clean and shut the kitchen down."

He shook his head, tapped the steering wheel anxiously with his fingers. "This is not how I expected things to end for us. So abruptly like this. I thought we had more time."

"So did I. But we both knew the end of our stay was coming sooner rather than later."

He nodded. "Why do you think she didn't tell you earlier?"

Angel sighed. A part of her believed Jillian had done this

purposefully, out of envy. Jillian didn't like that she and Everett had grown so close, and this was her spiteful way of plunging the knife in and giving it a good twist. But Angel was uncomfortable with the idea of bad-mouthing her boss to Everett. "That's just her way," she said simply.

"Well, I don't appreciate it. She should have been more considerate of you."

Angel couldn't help but scoff. "That would have been nice," she said, struggling to keep the sarcasm out of her voice. "I don't disagree but . . ."

"You could stay with me at the house until I leave for Europe."

"I wish." She shook her head. "The Harrisons arranged for me to take off work a little longer to help her out. Once she goes back home, I'm due back."

"How would your employer even know if you took off for a few extra days?"

"If I don't fly back with her tomorrow morning, I have no doubt she'll call my boss as soon as she gets home."

He shook his head, reached for her hand, and cupped it in his. "Then come with me."

Her jaw dropped. Her eyes darted from the ocean to him, trying to make sense of his words. "Excuse me?"

"Come to Europe with me. I'll be in meetings and giving speeches during the day, but I'll have free time some evenings and on weekends. And there's plenty to keep you entertained in Brussels and London and . . ."

"What?" she asked again as she tried to wrap her head around what he was saying.

"Why not? I don't want this to end now. Do you?"

"I . . ." Of course she didn't, but what he was suggesting was impossible. Out of the question. At least for her. She wiggled her fingers from his grasp. "You can't be serious."

"I'm dead serious. Why wouldn't I be?"

She looked back toward the ocean, not sure how to respond. Her feelings were all over the place. On the one hand it seemed like a dream that he was asking her to take off with him. But then she was annoyed that he would even suggest something so life-altering so offhandedly. Had he even given thought to what it would really mean for her? "I can't just drop everything and run off to Europe with you. I don't have it like that."

He was silent; she could see that he was taken aback by her response, a response he clearly was not expecting. "I . . . I'm not sure I understand what the problem is. You would be with me."

Now she was going from annoyed to thoroughly pissed. He really thought she could easily drop everything and take off on a whim. He had no clue of the huge implications that such actions would cause for her. She fixed her gaze on him. "You don't get it," she said, the aggravation mounting in her voice. "I have a job back home that I actually need to keep. I have commitments—a mortgage, bills to pay. And a skinny bank account with about $500 in savings to my name. If I take off for an extended absence, I'll get fired. What happens then? Have you thought about that?" She doubted it.

The look on his face indicated that the limitations of her life were finally beginning to dawn on him. "I get what you're saying. What if I speak to your employer and get him to give you a little more time off?"

She paused, unsure of just how her boss back home would react to a call from Everett Bruce. He might be flattered, but if she knew him like she thought she did, he would more likely be annoyed about her trying to get yet more time off from work. He had a busy, popular restaurant to run.

She shook her head firmly. "He's never going to give me more time off. It's already been way more than usual. He's called me twice the past week asking how much longer I thought I would need."

Everett sat quietly as awareness seemed to sink in. "I'm sorry. I didn't think about all of that."

Of course he hadn't. He didn't need to. "Look, I came at you kind of hard but I appreciate what you're trying to do."

"No. I deserved it. I was only thinking of my own feelings and my own life. I should have been more sensitive about what I'm suggesting would mean for you. It was selfish of me." He paused. "But don't give up on us yet," he said, starting the car. "I'll think of something."

10

Everett's words reverberated in Angel's ears as she cooked, cleaned, and packed for the trip back home. All the while she agonized over whether she'd made the right choice to end things with him.

Come with me.

She swallowed hard, her eyes fixated on the little blue seashells in the carpet in her room as she ran the vacuum over it. A part of her wondered why not just do that? Why not run off with him? What was the worst possible thing that could happen? Yes, she could lose her job, in fact, likely *would* lose it. But she was confident she could find another one quickly enough if it came to that. She had mad cooking skills, if she said so herself.

Of course, Everett could very well dump her at some point. But that was what living life fully was all about, wasn't it? Taking chances. One of her favorite sayings was that it was better to have loved and lost than to never have loved at all. Whatever the exact wording, she believed the sentiment to be one thousand percent true. Meanwhile, the thought of all the exhilarating possibilities for traveling the world and trying new things with him was inspiring. She was falling in love with a wonderful, powerful man, who was very much into her. Although neither of them had uttered the L-word—perhaps out of caution due to the temporary nature of vacationing on this paradise of an island—it felt like he was crazy about her. So many women would jump at the chance to take him up on his unbelievable offer, even at the risk of ending up heartbroken and losing everything.

Still, she couldn't simply toss aside all the years, decades really, that it had taken to claw her way up to the job of sous-chef at a very popular restaurant in Washington, DC. Or the time and sacrifices required to scrimp and save enough for the down payment on her condo. She could remember canceling all but the most basic TV services and holding on to computers and cell phones until they crashed. She couldn't count the number of unrecoverable blank screens she had faced. If things didn't work out between her and Everett, if he got bored and sent her on her way, she could lose both her livelihood and her home. Or what if he turned out not to be the man he seemed to be, and she decided to leave him? She shook her head as she vacuumed around the edges of the bed. It was too risky.

Or was it? Dammit! She was so confused.

She stopped vacuuming and stared into space, her mind racing. She had looked into his business dealings online but not much into his personal life. It hadn't seemed necessary, especially after he'd opened up to her about his late wife. She'd always assumed that her relationship with Everett was likely a passionate summer fling, as much as she'd hoped otherwise. That the reality was that once they left the island, they would both go their separate ways. But now that she was entertaining the idea of leaving so much behind to be with him, she needed to know as much as possible.

She shut off the vacuum cleaner and sat on the edge of her bed, between the two half-full suitcases. On her laptop, she typed *Everett and Chloe Bruce* into the browser search bar. URLs spread down the screen before her. The list was short, much shorter than the one that had popped up when she'd googled him alone and had gotten everything related to his business and philanthropic dealings. Maybe that was to be expected since the two had been married for only four years when Chloe died.

The first several listings led to articles and social media posts about their wedding day. Apparently, Chloe's parents had doled out nearly a half-million dollars for the extravagant affair. Then the couple honeymooned on the islands of French Polynesia, including Bora-Bora and Tahiti. Following that, they'd returned home and purchased the humongous $50 million, thirty-thousand-square-foot gated property on the Potomac River, which they'd christened Riverwild Estate. A handful of pieces discussed the couple's generous donations to social causes under a foundation founded by Everett, the Bruce Fund. They'd both served on several boards and sponsored internships promoting education for underserved students, primarily African Americans.

Scrolling further, Angel was surprised to come across a piece in the *Washington Post*, this one about Chloe's death, titled "Wife of Powerful Investor Everett Bruce Commits Suicide in Her Home." Seeing the words spelled out right there in front of her made the moment all too real. She sank down onto the floor with her laptop and devoured each and every word of the brief description of what happened that night.

Apparently, Chloe had shot herself in the heart. The reporter had interviewed the police, Everett, and his older sister, Ida, as well as Chloe's parents, who were utterly despondent. Understandably. But Angel had not expected to learn that her parents were also full of doubts about how it all had gone down. They had refused to accept that their daughter would ever have held a gun anywhere near her body. They insisted that Chloe was fearful of guns. Her father had pleaded with the police to dig deeper, despite who Everett was, to little avail. "No man is above the law," her father had repeated often to anyone who'd listen. Still, the case had been closed rather quickly, and Chloe's death ruled accidental. According to another more recent article, six months after Chloe's death her dad had died in the hospital of serious head injuries suffered from a fall down the stairs in his home. Her mom believed he had just given up due to profound grief.

Angel shut her laptop, took a deep breath. The details were chilling. The whole affair had been crushingly heartbreaking for Chloe's parents; she had been their only child, and Angel's heart went out to them. Even though she had never met the couple, she could certainly understand why it was so hard on them. Yet everything she'd just read in the *Post*, as well as two smaller local publications about that horrible day, lined up with what Everett had told her. They'd argued. He'd left the room only to return and see Chloe lying on the floor dead of a gunshot wound.

Angel stood up. It had been an appalling tragedy; she only hoped Chloe's mother had somehow eventually found peace. But Everett had been honest with her about that night. She was thankful for that.

So why not throw her fears to the wind and take a chance with this man? He had a way of making her feel safe and protected. And so very special. She picked up her cell phone to dial Dawn, one of her best friends from childhood, whose wedding she had recently attended, and the only one from home she'd let in on whom she'd been seeing on the island. And even with Dawn, she had shared just the bare bones. Her friend was unaware of how far the relationship had progressed. But Dawn was practical, and Angel knew she could count on getting a no-nonsense response. Angel felt in desperate need of advice from someone she trusted before making such a monumental decision about her future.

Before she could put the call through, the doorbell rang. Jillian had invited two of her sorority sisters who owned houses in Oak Bluffs and always stayed until late fall to drop in for afternoon tea. Angel had baked French madeleines for the occasion.

Jillian and her girlfriends planned to gather for one last hurrah before Jillian left for home. Angel stood and walked to her bedroom door to shut it but paused at the sound of one of the voices drifting up the staircase. It was not a woman, as expected. It was the husky voice of a man. A man whose voice she had come to know very well. Everett Bruce.

She froze in her spot, dazed. Everett was there at the house? Impossible. She tiptoed into the hallway, trying to get a little closer to the stairs to be sure she'd heard right. She realized immediately that it was indeed him. She couldn't decipher the words being spoken, but she could clearly make out Jillian's excitable gushing.

Beads of sweat popped out on her forehead; her stomach turned into a ball of knots. What should she do? What was *he* doing? What was he thinking? It had been only a few hours since she'd left him that morning. And now he was here? She dashed back into her room and paced, attempting to make sense of it all. She heard Jillian calling her from the bottom of the stairs and froze, needing time to think. Then she realized she could not keep ignoring her name. She walked to the top of the stairs, too leery to venture farther, and looked down to see Jillian standing there, a very puzzled half smile on her face.

"You called, Mrs. Harrison?"

"Angel, dear," Jillian exclaimed. "Everett Bruce is here to see you. He says he wants to talk."

"Um, I'll be right down."

She dashed back into her room, grabbed tissues, blotted her face dry. Then she took a deep breath, slipped out, and descended the stairs. Everett was standing at the entrance to the sitting room, alongside Jillian. Out of the corner of her eye, Angel could see Jillian's friends Cora and Sabrina sitting on the far side of the room.

"Angel," Everett said, moving forward the moment he saw her.

"Everett." She tried to smile. "What's this all about?"

He turned toward her employer. "Jillian, if you don't mind, I need to speak to Angel in private. Is there another room we can use?"

Jillian's eyes grew wide; she seemed speechless for a second but quickly managed to find her voice. "Um, yes. You can use the solarium. Right this way." She led them both down the hall to a large, sunny room decorated in white and yellow. As soon as Jillian shut the French doors, Everett took Angel's hand into his, got down on one knee.

Angel gasped and tried to pull him back up. "What in the world are you doing, Everett? This is . . ."

"Just listen for now, Angel," he said. She stopped tugging, quieting down.

"I've given this a lot of thought and I've made up my mind." She stared in disbelief as he whipped a small box from the pocket of his khaki pants. He popped it open, revealing the largest, glitteriest, most sparkling diamond ring she'd ever seen. Her hands flew to her mouth. She wanted to speak but the wind had been knocked clear out of her being.

"Marry me, Angel," he said, pulling on her left hand. "Over the past several weeks, you have become everything to me. I don't want what we have together to end. Ever. I want you to be my wife."

"Everett . . . Oh, God. I don't know what to say. I . . ."

"Say yes. This should erase any doubts or fears you have about me. Or about us. Or your future. You'll travel with me to Europe, then return with me to Riverwild. I love you. I want us to grow old together. To have children together."

Only minutes ago, she had been seriously thinking of running off with him. And that was without a ring or a proposal. Now she had both. So what the hell was she waiting for?

"Yes. Yes, I'll marry you."

His smile was as wide as the sunroom as he slipped the ring onto her finger. He stood and they embraced warmly. "I can't believe you finally said yes. Took you long enough."

"I can't believe you actually asked me. But I do love you, Everett. So very much."

"You've made me happier than I've ever been, you know. Our time here has been precious to me, some of the best days of my life."

She smiled. "Mine, too." She had no idea what she was throwing herself into. She just knew that the past weeks had been her most fulfilling. Everett had a way of making her feel like the most cherished person on the planet. He was sweet, attentive, loving. And filthy rich. What more could she ask for? Not a thing. What was that saying? It was just as easy to love a rich man as a poor one. Or something like that. Was this risky? Heck, yes. But it felt so right.

"Should we tell the others now?" he asked.

Oh, that, Angel thought, growing a little apprehensive at the idea of going out and announcing to the world that Everett had proposed to her. Especially Jillian. She tightened her lips as the reality washed over her. She really was going to become Mrs. Everett Bruce. The prospect was daunting but also stimulating when she thought more about what it actually meant. About all the ways her life was about to change, as well as the unknowns. She would obviously leave this job with the Harrisons. She so much enjoyed coming to the island every summer, despite Mrs. Harrison's finicky and condescending ways. Still, she couldn't imagine leaving her future husband to come here and work every summer. But what about her job at Georgia's back at home? And her condo? Would she keep those? She loved them both dearly. Had worked so hard to acquire them. They would not be easy to give up.

Her head started to swirl. She didn't drink much, but this

moment seemed to call for a shot of something. She looked into Everett's eyes and immediately felt calmer. She would have to pace herself, to take this all one day at a time. For now, she would focus on what was directly in front of her.

"Yes," she said. "Let's do it."

* * *

For once, Jillian had not a word to say. At least momentarily. Everett announced their engagement as the couple held hands, Angel gripping his tightly for dear life. You could have pierced the air with the sharp silence running through the sitting room. Jillian stood awkwardly in the middle of the floor, her eyelashes batting a mile a minute as her two girlfriends stood close behind. The three of them, in their flowery little sundresses, stared at the couple in total disbelief.

Finally one of them found the appropriate words. "Congratulations to you both," Cora said, an awkward smile gracing her lips. "I'm so happy for you, Angel."

"Yes, congratulations," Sabrina said, with a small, nervous laugh.

Jillian did not even attempt a smile as she shifted from one foot to the other. "Well. I . . . I must say I had no idea this was coming."

"Of course you didn't," Everett said. "I admit it's sudden." He looked at Angel. "But we're very happy."

Angel smiled tensely, eyeing Jillian closely. Waiting for the curt comment, the biting glare so common from her boss.

"I almost feel I should thank you," Everett said.

"Whatever for?" Jillian asked, frowning.

"For hiring her to work here on the island. Otherwise, we would never have met."

"Hmm," Jillian said, clasping her hands together. "How true. Well. Congratulations."

"Thank you," they said in unison. It was more than obvious that their engagement had thrown Jillian for a big loop, Angel thought. It had thrown *her* for a loop. She felt a little sorry for Jillian, having to deal with the news that Everett saw his future in Angel, rather than her daughter. Or any of the women in her circle. Jillian probably found it incomprehensible. But Angel also had to admit she felt a certain glee at watching her boss do the squirming for once. In the end, Jillian would land on her feet. Women like her always did.

"We understand this will come as a surprise to many," Everett said.

"Yes, it's a shocker," Jillian said. She cleared her throat.

"Have you decided on a date?" Cora asked, looking at Everett.

Everett glanced at Angel. "We haven't talked about that yet. It's up to her."

Angel shook her head. One thing at a time, she thought. "No. Not yet."

"But she will be coming to Europe with me when I leave next week."

"I assume you have a place to stay until then, Angel," Jillian said. "Since I'm leaving in the morning."

"She'll be staying with me, starting tonight." Everett glanced at Angel. "Right?"

Everything had happened so quickly that Angel hadn't given any thought to where she would park her weary, newly engaged head that night. "Yes," she said.

"Then she'll accompany me to Europe," he said. "I have business there."

"Of course," Jillian said quietly. The usual elation in Jillian's demeanor when Everett was around had disappeared. Angel could see Jillian's expression droop more and more as she seemed to truly grasp what was happening. Jillian cleared her throat. "How wonderful for you both. Will you live at Riverwild Estate?"

He nodded.

"I guess this means you'll no longer work for us over the summer then, Angel? No, of course not. Why would you?" Jillian chuckled tensely.

Angel cleared her throat. But what she really wanted was to clear the air and get out of there. "I'll go up and finish packing now, I guess . . ."

Everett squeezed Angel's hand. "No need for you to do that, sweetheart. I'll get someone to gather your things for you."

Jillian arched her brows. "Naturally."

Angel touched him on the arm. "No, really. You don't need to do that. I can finish up."

"Then I'll wait and load everything into the car when you're done."

Angel shook her head. "You should go on back to the house. Just give me a couple of hours. I'll get a cab to your place." She was ready for this awkwardness among the three of them to end. The sooner he left and she followed, the better.

"At least let me send a driver for you." He glanced at his watch. "Say five o'clock?"

She nodded. "That should work. That will allow me time to tidy up the kitchen."

"Nonsense," Jillian said. "We can't have the future wife of Everett Bruce clearing up a kitchen, can we? I'll get someone else to do it, dear. Now let me get a look at that rock on your finger."

Angel held up her hand, barely able to believe she'd heard her boss right. Jillian was going to hire someone else to do her job?

"Lovely," Jillian said. "And I can also help you finish packing."

"We appreciate that," Everett said.

Angel said nothing as she tried to digest the words coming out of her boss's mouth. Jillian had never offered to help her with anything in all the years she'd worked there. If this were a hint as to how she would be treated by others as Everett's wife, she had no complaints.

Everett kissed her goodbye at the door, and true to her word, Jillian followed her up to the tiny room in back of the house to help pack after bidding her friends a quick goodbye. Angel realized as they squeezed inside that this was the first time she could remember Jillian entering her bedroom, other than when she'd showed her around the house that first summer. Angel hadn't expected anything palatial as a servant but had been a bit taken off guard by the diminutive size when she'd first laid eyes on it.

She went to the dresser drawer where she kept her cotton pajamas and nighties, gathered the contents, and placed them on the bed between the suitcases.

Jillian picked up a nightgown and slowly began to refold it to her liking. "If this goes through, you'll need an entire new wardrobe." She chuckled.

If this goes through? "Really, Mrs. Harrison," Angel said, watching as Jillian folded at a snail's pace. "I can manage. There's not much more to do."

"Nonsense. I said I would help. I meant it." Jillian placed the nightgown into a suitcase. "It's the least I can do, considering."

"Considering?" Angel grabbed a pair of well-worn tennis shoes from the bottom of her closet.

"Well, you know. With the upcoming nuptials. I mean, you're marrying Everett Bruce. Have you even started planning?"

"No. This just happened."

"And you had no idea he was about to pop the question?"

Angel frowned, beginning to suspect that Jillian was really here to pry. She should have known. "None. When he asked me to go to Europe with him before he proposed, I said no."

Jillian stared at Angel like she'd just seen a ghost. "Everett invited you to Europe and you turned him down?"

"It felt too chancy to give everything up and go off with a man I'm not married or engaged to."

Jillian clapped her hands slowly and dramatically. "You played that masterfully, Angel."

Angel stopped trying to stuff the sneakers into the sides of her suitcase and looked up at Jillian. "Excuse me?"

"You got him to propose."

Angel could not believe this woman. "It's not like that. I never expected him . . . You know what?" She grabbed the pajama top out of Jillian's hands and shoved it into one of the bags. Then she took Jillian's arm and hastily steered her toward the door. She had put up with the smart-ass mouth and superior attitude for the last time.

"I can finish this by myself," Angel said.

"But I was going to offer some advice and suggestions for a wedding planner for you and . . ."

"I'll be in touch if I need your help." Angel gave Jillian one final gentle shove. Jillian turned to face her just outside the door.

"Angel, you have no idea what you're getting yourself into with this marriage. Or the demands that will be placed on you as Mrs. Everett Bruce. Do you know anything at all about his estate, Riverwild? The size and complexity will do you in. Even *I* would feel intimidated at the prospect of living there."

"He has servants to take care of those things."

"Absolutely he does, but he'll expect you to be responsible for making sure it all runs smoothly."

Angel had to admit the prospect of taking on Riverwild in any capacity was intimidating. She'd seen the pictures in the *Post*. The estate was enormous, with gardens, fountains, tennis courts, a massive swimming pool. She and Everett had only touched on running it, and she knew his sister, Ida, was very much involved. How much Angel would handle remained to be decided.

Then there was the short amount of time she'd known Everett.

Jillian didn't seem bothered at all by that. He was rich, so Jillian no doubt assumed he must be perfect and that if anyone might cause issues in the relationship, it would be Angel. She'd be deceiving herself if she didn't admit that the newness of the relationship had crossed her mind a few times. But she was always able to quickly brush any worries aside, given the way he made her feel so cherished and safe.

Everything about this whole darn venture she was about to embark on was unnerving. She couldn't dwell on that. If she did, she might very well chicken out.

Of course, Jillian wasn't exactly sharing her concerns out of empathy. Out of envy would be more like it. And Angel refused to let this woman get to her, ever again. From now on she was going to try to surround herself with people who uplifted her, not those who tore her down.

"I'm sure I'll be fine," Angel said as she shut the door, right in Jillian's face. Jillian gasped so loudly Angel could hear it. Then, instead of folding her clothes as she had been, she threw them all into the suitcases. She wanted out of this house as fast as possible. She was so ready to leave all this behind, dust in her wake, to start her new life. It couldn't possibly be any worse than this. She would dearly miss the warm sandy beaches, the splendid sunsets, the soothing ocean breezes. She would *not* miss her rude, offensive employer.

She really had little idea what the future would bring for her at Riverwild, but the one comfort was knowing that she was embarking upon the unknown with Everett—her protector, her lover, her future husband. She had faith that he would get her through anything that lay ahead.

Part 2

11

Forcing one eye open, Angel found herself squinting hard against a garishly bright sliver of early-morning sunlight poking around the edges of the floor-to-ceiling drapes. She stretched leisurely across the king-size bed as her vision adjusted to the surroundings. The bespoke French furniture, posh embroidered fabrics, and porcelain lamps reminded her how far away this swanky hotel on the right bank of the Seine was from her little condo in DC. Especially from the tiny bedroom in the Harrison house. Not only in distance but also in lifestyle. The contrasts were mind-blowing.

The first time she'd stepped off the private elevator and into one of the suites where they'd stayed over the past month, she had actually exclaimed at the sight of the baby grand piano sitting majestically in a corner of one of the sitting rooms. She asked Everett if he played.

"Oh no, but it's nice, isn't it?" Neither did she, but it was so pretty she wished she did. She'd stared at the impressive instrument, tempted to run her fingers across the ivory-colored keys.

Everett had clearly sensed her curiosity. "Go ahead. Try it out."

"So afraid I'll break something," she said, only half joking.

114 | Connie Briscoe

"Don't be."

She sat and hit a couple keys, then quickly stood back up when their private butler entered the room carrying a tray of refreshments. She didn't want to make a spectacle of herself.

So far on the trip she had never seen Everett pay a bill, at least not in her presence. He never stopped at a hotel front desk, never touched a single piece of luggage. He was greeted at every entrance and whisked off to his suite directly from the chauffeured car that was always waiting when his private jet landed. Such a life, she thought. It was going to take her a while to get used to it all. Sometimes she wondered if she ever would. Had Chloe ever felt so out of place? As if this kind of existence might be too much? Probably not. She had been so classy, so perfect from the start. She probably had slid into the lifestyle effortlessly.

Angel lifted her left hand from beneath the sheets and quickly scanned it, homing in on the ring finger. This had become a morning ritual of late to make sure she wasn't dreaming. The big hunk of a diamond still glowed spectacularly.

She rolled over to face the other side of the bed, now empty. Everett had long since hit the streets of Paris, having left the room at six thirty that morning for a business meeting after brushing her forehead with a tender kiss. Also a morning ritual. It had been the same in London, Brussels, Frankfurt. Something she had realized over the past four weeks during this trip, with more than a little regret: her soon-to-be husband was a workaholic. He was nothing like the leisurely good-time Everett she'd spent countless hours roaming around with on Martha's Vineyard.

"You can't say I didn't warn you that I would be extremely busy here," he'd said over lunch at a popular brasserie before heading back to the office the morning after they'd hit London, their first destination. "Work hard so you can play hard. That's my motto."

She had fiddled with the shepherd's pie that he had encouraged her to try as she took in his words. "But that was before, you know, you got engaged." She pointed at the rock on her finger. "You're about to get married now. Start a family. Remember?"

He'd smiled and nodded. "All in due time, love. My workload isn't always this heavy. But while I'm here, I have to make the most of it."

She really hoped that was the case. That he did not always work so darn much, but she wasn't convinced. Waking up all these weeks and looking across the bed to see a bare pillow had to be the loneliest feeling in the world. It was obvious that he loved what he did, and, of course, she was tremendously proud of his many accomplishments. He was one of the most successful Black men in America. Heck, one of the most successful, period. That was a big reason why she found him so attractive. She often wished her parents were still around to meet him, to see how far their daughter had come. Especially her dad. She had a feeling he and Everett would have hit it off.

She slipped out of bed, pulled on a silk knee-length robe, then strolled toward the private flower-decked terrace that ran the length of the suite. Along the way she passed by a large black-and-white painting of a smiling Josephine Baker, the Black American-born entertainer who took Paris by storm in the 1920s and eventually settled there. The portrait was one of the reasons that this was Everett's favorite suite at the hotel, and she loved being greeted by it every morning.

Everett, thoughtful as always, had instructed the butler to serve her coffee and juice when she got up at nine. That much hadn't changed. He stepped onto the terrace and poured a cup while she peered over the railing, soaking up the sights on the streets below, as Parisians dashed around to begin their days.

"Can I get you anything else?" he asked.

She smiled. "That's all for now, thank you, Andre."

"Very well."

"On second thought," she said just before he slipped back in-side, "can I get a breakfast menu?" Why not, now that someone else was doing the cooking?

"Of course, ma'am."

She sat at the table and sipped her coffee as Andre exited. It was the same brand she had raved about in Edgartown, and now it was served to her in every city they touched. She leaned back in the chair, closed her eyes. It had been a dream of hers to visit the City of Light since forever, and here she was, vacationing with a man and in a manner far beyond her wildest dreams. After a stay at the house in Edgartown with Everett, where they'd spent a week shopping for a new wardrobe and set of luggage for her, the couple had hopped aboard his Gulf Stream jet and flown to London. Then it was on to several other cities Angel had fantasized about seeing someday, finally ending up here in Paris. Visiting even one of these destinations would have been a dream come true, and here she was exploring them all with her fiancé.

Everything was so perfect, except for one thing. And it was a biggie. Everett's rigid, round-the-clock work habits. He usually got up around five to take business calls from people halfway across the globe. Then he showered, dressed, and took a car to his office in the financial district of whichever city they were in. By the time he returned to the hotel, it was often eight or nine in the evening. Depending on how tired he was, they would dine out or most often, eat in. Once in a while he would leave work early and take her to an attraction that he knew she would enjoy, like the afternoon he'd surprised her in London with tickets to Kew Gardens. They had spent a leisurely three hours strolling through the lush, colorful flowers and trees.

Sadly, though, that kind of thing was rare. Most days he

worked, worked, worked. Gone was the guy in Martha's Vineyard who'd had loads of free time. She truly missed that man. Now she was expected to find ways to entertain herself. Alone. She was no clothes horse and could only spend so much time shopping. Fortunately, there was no shortage of sites and activities in the bustling locales where they had traveled. Still, it got lonely, and one afternoon she'd gone on a group walking tour through Frankfurt simply to have company.

She had finally won Everett over, in a way, during dinner the previous evening at a trendy restaurant in Paris. She'd turned on all her charms to get him to come out and dine with her after his twelve-hour workday, hinting that she had an idea she wanted to discuss with him.

"Now what did you have in mind?" he'd asked, stifling a yawn as soon as the waiter departed.

"Am I that boring?" she had teased.

He reached across the table and took her hand. "Of course not. There's nothing I like more than to spend my days with you. You know that."

"I really appreciate you taking the time to come here tonight, as exhausted as you are."

His cell phone chimed for the second time since they'd sat down. He groaned and picked it up from the table. She sighed with annoyance and leaned back in her chair, keeping her thoughts to herself. Otherwise, she might get to cursing.

She was surprised to see him quickly place the phone back onto the table. "That can wait," he said without answering.

"Oh, cool. Now how about turning it off? At least until we finish here?"

He was quiet for a few seconds, then flipped the button on his phone. "There. Silenced."

"Thank you." It made her feel good that he would do that.

"So, you've got my undivided attention. I'm dying to hear what you wanted to say."

"Let's stay here in Paris for an extra few days before we go home to Riverwild." They had been planning to fly back to the States in two days.

"I thought you were excited to see Riverwild."

"Oh, I am. I can barely wait." It was true. She'd heard so much about the mystical place. "But Paris has always been a dream of mine. I want more time to explore. There's so much to see. Like the Louvre."

"I thought you went there."

"I did but the place is huge. You can't see it all in one day. And what's the name of that Shakespeare bookstore?"

He nodded. "Shakespeare and Company. I agree. You should see that."

"*We* should see it. Together. And if we stay, no more work for you. You're hanging out with me, like we did on Martha's Vineyard."

He smiled silently. She could tell he was mulling the idea over.

"Only for a few more days," she added. "Then we head home."

"Okay," he said finally.

She clapped, barely able to believe he was agreeing. "Really?"

"I can't promise there won't be a single business call, but I can't think of a better way to end this business trip than to spend some time touring Paris with you. It'll be fun."

Andre stepped onto the patio bearing a tray filled with fresh fruit and breakfast pastries, set them out carefully on the table before her, and left. So now it was the last day of Angel and Everett's extended stay in Paris, yet here she was sitting on the terrace of the hotel room all by her lonesome self. So far, Everett had been able to get away from work and join her for only a few hours. That had been enough time to check the bookstore and a tiny corner of a museum that was one of the largest in the world. She had heard it could take a month to see the tens of thousands of works of art at the Louvre.

She was deeply disappointed and let him know it. He'd tried to make up for it by arranging a private tour of the Louvre and promising to join her for dinner at a really nice restaurant that evening. She glanced at her watch and realized she had only an hour before the museum tour was to start. She would have to finish breakfast and dress quickly.

At dinner that night, Everett pulled out all the stops to try and make up for his absences. The restaurant he chose was one of those fancy deals where the waiter flipped the white cloth napkin ceremoniously across her lap. But the kicker was when they brought out a little black leather stool and placed it near her seat. She looked at Everett, made a puzzled expression that said "What am I supposed to do with that?"

Everett leaned across the table. "It's for your purse," he said softly.

"Oh? Really?" As she placed it on the stool, Angel was so thankful that Everett had taken her shopping for a nice, soft leather designer bag before they left Edgartown. It would have been embarrassing to have placed one of her well-worn cotton totes there. She glanced at the waiter. If he had heard the exchange, you would never know it. His expression remained staid as he approached the table and asked if they were having drinks before dinner.

Everett asked for the sommelier and expertly questioned him about the wine selection. As always, tiny little chills ran up her arm. He was so obviously in his milieu and looked so suave. She supposed she should be more appreciative of this life he was giving her. In only a month, she had seen more of Europe than she could ever have imagined she would see in a lifetime. More than most people saw over their lifetimes. And she was doubly blessed to have visited without a budget. Private jets, luxury hotels, sumptuous spa treatments, five-star restaurants. She felt a little shameful about ever complaining. But honestly, if anyone had asked what she had enjoyed more, the four weeks visiting Europe or the six weeks on Martha's Vineyard, she would have responded without a second's hesitation: Martha's Vineyard. Those days had been a dream, mainly because she'd had Everett's undivided devotion and attention.

Back in the hotel suite she strolled toward the bedroom as Everett walked off to the den, his cell phone glued to his ear. Warm memories of an evening filled with laughter and delicious food filled her thoughts as she slipped out of her heels. Passing by the bed on her way to the dressing room, she noted that one of the new silk nightgowns she'd purchased on their first afternoon in Paris had been spread out by one of the many hotel assistants always tending to their needs. It had been the same in every hotel they'd stayed in. She should be used to it all by now, but still it felt odd, almost intrusive. Maybe she wanted to pick out her own nightie. When she had mentioned this to Everett, he'd chuckled and said, "Let them do their job. You'll get used to it."

He entered the bedroom, his necktie loosened, his phone nowhere to be seen, for once. He smiled as he crossed the carpet and took her hands. She smiled, too. She loved it when he focused solely on her. That seemed to happen less and less since leaving the island. Hopefully that would change when they got back to the States.

"One more thing before you get busy, future Mrs. Bruce," he said. He bent down, scooped up her slippers from the side of the bed, and handed them to her. Then he guided her out to the terrace. This all reminded her of the old Everett. The attentive, considerate, charming one. The one she wished would show up more often these days.

It was a clear night, the dark sky filled with a zillion stars twinkling brightly above them. "What is it?" she asked, anticipation getting the better of her.

And then he did it. Got down on one knee just as he had at the Harrison house in Oak Bluffs. She stared at him in silence. Now she was really puzzled.

"Let's get married as soon as we get back, love."

She blinked. "You mean . . . like go to the justice of the peace?" she finally managed.

"Not that. I can get someone to come to the house. Better yet, rather than spring this on my sister and the staff at the last minute, we can stay in a hotel in DC for one or two nights. I'll get a marriage officiant to come to us. Marry us there."

She frowned. "But why? What's the rush, Everett? I don't get it."

He stood up and sighed. "This isn't going quite as smoothly as I planned," he said, chuckling. "Why wait six months or a year or whatever? If we know this is what we want, why not go ahead and do it now?"

She mulled over his words. Yes, she knew she wanted to be with this man forever. She adored him to the heavens and back. He was everything to her, so no problem there. But a quickie wedding? That she wasn't so sure about. She'd been looking forward to trying on gorgeous gowns, searching for a picturesque venue, deciding on cakes and flowers and the menu, and all the other pomp and circumstance that went into planning a big wedding.

"I'm excited about preparing for the whole thing," she said. "I've never been married before. I want to do it right. That takes time. And don't you want your sister and friends to be there?"

He nodded. "Of course, but we can always throw a nice reception in a few months' time or whenever you want. I really do think it will be a lot better for you to arrive home with me as my wife."

So that was what this was about. She laughed. "You mean, rather than as your lover? Or the fiancée you've known for only a couple of months? Wait a second. You told Ida, right?"

"Slow down with the twenty questions. No, I have not told my sister. Not yet."

"You can't be serious. You said you were going to let her know before we left the island."

"Did I? I guess I don't remember saying that."

Angel stared at him in disbelief. This was bizarre. He had absolutely said it. His sister lived at Riverwild. They were flying back tomorrow. And he hadn't yet told her they were getting married? She'd called and told her two best friends, Dawn and Patrice, about the proposal within hours. "Why haven't you told her, Everett?"

"I just . . . haven't gotten around to it."

"Well, when do you plan . . . ?"

"Before we get back."

She was completely perplexed about his lackadaisical attitude when it came to telling Ida. "What will she think about you re-marrying so soon and waiting so long to tell her?"

"Honestly? It's hard to say. But it doesn't really matter."

"Of course it matters. She's your sister."

He shook his head firmly. "Not really. I mean, yes, she's my big sister and protective at times but . . ."

"How old is she?"

"Forty-eight, three years older than me. But it's you I'm marrying. You're the one who will be Mrs. Bruce."

Those words made her heart sing. "Mrs. Bruce," she said, smiling. "I do like the sound of that."

"Then why wait? We can get married as soon as we get back. Somehow it feels like it will be easier to announce all this if it's a done deal. If you're already my wife."

She inhaled deeply, then let it all out. "Okay. Okay. If that's what you want." Why fight it? She was thrilled that he was anxious to get hitched.

He took her in his arms, kissed her, then dipped her playfully. She laughed as he pulled his cell phone from his pocket and walked toward the den. "Let me make a couple of quick calls to my assistant to get the ball rolling and have everything set up for when we arrive in DC. Love you."

"Love you back."

As soon as he disappeared through the doorway, she screamed silently into her fists. She danced wildly up and down the length of the terrace as if she were a teenager. This really was beyond exciting. It was exhilarating, electrifying, enthralling.

She sank down onto a lounge chair, her chest heaving wildly as she leaned back to catch her breath. How had this happened? A few months ago, she was a sous-chef in a restaurant. Now she was about to marry a billionaire. Her life was going to change enormously. Forever. She'd known that, of course, the day Everett had proposed and she'd accepted. Now that it truly was about to happen, the reality was hitting her like a stack of bricks. Not only were a bunch of new things about to become a part of her life—like private jets and megamansions and servants galore— she would also have to leave a lot behind. Her job, her condo, her trusty little red Honda. Life as she'd known it.

At first, she had resolved that that was the way it had to be. If she wanted to marry Everett, she had to take the sour with the sweet. And let's face it, the sweet wasn't just good; it was astounding. Enough to take her breath away. But she could not let all that had been dear in her old life go just like that. Some things she needed to hold on to for the sake of sanity. Like her closest friends, Dawn and Patrice. Or some of the posters and sculptures in her condo that she had collected over the years. Even if they were nothing like the priceless artwork Everett owned, they were still precious to her. She was determined to find a place for them amid all the finery at Riverwild Estate.

And then there was her cooking. Working as a chef hadn't been just a way to earn a living for her; it was a way of being. She loved cooking, couldn't imagine her life without it. She had already touched on this with Everett, telling him to expect her to spend time here and there in the kitchen at Riverwild whipping up some of the dishes from the long-neglected cookbook she had been working on. He did not understand this at all. There was a world-class chef at the mansion who would prepare anything and everything her heart desired, he kept reminding her.

"Oh, yeah?" she had teased. "Even some chitterlings?"

"You eat those things?" he had asked, staring at her as if he'd just seen a phantom.

"Once or twice a year, sure do. New Year's Day, Thanksgiving. They bring good luck."

"Well, count me out," he'd said with a chuckle. "My luck is plenty good."

"That's what you say now but you haven't tried *my* chitterlings. Just you wait."

She sat up at the sound of the terrace door opening. It was Andre with a bottle of cabernet sauvignon, the same brand that they'd had at dinner. The same brand that she'd liked enough to have a few glasses of. How Everett had managed to have a bottle pop up in their hotel suite a mere hour after they'd left, she had no idea. But she was learning to expect the unexpected when it came to her guy.

"Mr. Bruce said to tell you that he'll be right out, ma'am," Andre said as he placed the bottle and two long-stemmed glasses on the table. Along with the loveliest lavender-colored flower she'd ever seen.

"What kind of flower is that, Andre?"

He smiled. "A sterling rose, ma'am," he said, then backed out of the room.

She took a long, generous swig while waiting for her future husband—her *very-near*-future husband—to return. In a matter of days, she would become Mrs. Everett Bruce and they would be on their way to Riverwild Estate.

12

The moment the black sedan breezed through the wrought iron gates and began the half-mile drive to the mansion, Angel and Everett both fell silent. They had been chatting enthusiastically about their wedding the day before, held in their suite in a luxury hotel in Washington, DC. One of Everett's assistants had arranged for a local designer to bring several off-white gowns to the room, and Angel had picked out a short, lacy number. A seamstress altered the dress until it fit her like a glove.

Everett had the hotel decorate the lavish suite with elegant lavender and white candles and create a bouquet for Angel of the sterling roses she had come to love ever since first laying eyes on them in Paris. The roses, believed to symbolize love at first sight, had a sweet citrusy fragrance that filled the air and were the perfect complement. Two of Everett's business associates and their wives served as witnesses; champagne and music from a jazz trio flowed until they left at midnight. It had been a memorable, lively affair for something thrown together so quickly.

She'd barely had time to adjust to becoming a wife and now here she was being tossed headfirst into her new home, a thirty-thousand-square-foot mansion situated on ten wooded acres bordering the Potomac River. Her eyes darted around, trying to soak up every detail as they drove through a grove of perfectly manicured trees and shrubbery that looked like they could have been plucked out of a glossy horticulture magazine. Although deliriously happy, Angel at times felt like she was in an endless whirl, struggling to find a second to catch her breath. As they glided by a guardhouse, a caretaker's house, a guesthouse, and tennis courts, her palms grew clammier by the second. She thought her heart would pop out of her chest. Everett, holding her hand, clearly sensed the growing anxiety and gave a little reassuring squeeze. That helped soothe her senses, somewhat. She smiled at him.

Then they rounded another corner, and the magnificent four-story mansion sprang into view, seeming to float among the clouds. She sat back and exhaled as the car swerved into a decorated cobblestone courtyard with stairs leading up to two massive carved wooden doors. They had to be the biggest doors Angel had ever seen. She took the driver's extended hand and stepped from the car, her eyes still glued to the enormous structure towering in front of her. This was the house that she was now expected to call home? *That* was really going to take some getting used to, she thought while adjusting her navy woolen blazer across her shoulders. Mrs. Harrison and the couples at their wedding last night had raved about Riverwild, and the place was beautiful. But she was completely unprepared for the colossus spread out before her.

She tried to appear calm as Everett led the way up the wide staircase. The heavy doors swung open, and they stepped into a dimly lit vestibule as a Black man with a receding gray hairline and a stern smile stepped aside. He was dressed in a dark suit and red bow tie, and Angel knew immediately that this must be Jackson, the executive manager Everett had mentioned from time to time. He oversaw things at the house under Ida's watchful eye.

"Good afternoon, Mr. Bruce," he said, extending his hand. "Wonderful to have you back. I hope you enjoyed your time away."

"Jackson, good to see you. I definitely did. I want you to meet Mrs. Bruce. Angel, this is Jackson. He helps Ida keep things running smoothly around here." Angel barely heard a word as her eyes followed a long wrought-iron staircase winding up and around on its way to the second story.

"Angel," Everett repeated with a little nudge.

She snapped out of her trance. "Yes," she said, nodding. "Hello, Jackson."

He looked surprisingly fit and spry. From Everett's description of his graying hair, she had pictured someone in his fifties or older, but this man looked a decade younger. She wondered if she should shake his hand. To her relief, he extended a palm and smiled warmly.

"Hello, Mrs. Bruce. Welcome to Riverwild." Jackson glanced toward Everett. "And congratulations to you both. Ida informed me of your marriage after you telephoned her yesterday evening, Mr. Bruce."

At the sound of his welcoming voice, Angel felt some of the butterflies that had been fluttering around in her tummy since they'd first turned onto the driveway begin to settle down. She had the feeling she was going to like this Jackson.

In the next instant, she began to think she may have started getting comfy too soon. A tall, slender, stylishly dressed woman in navy slacks, a tan cashmere pullover with a strand of pearls, and trendy leather flats emerged from a side hallway. She wore her jet-black curls in a closely cut natural style. Hazel eyes, thick brows. She vaguely reminded Angel of a more feminine version of Everett. She knew instantly this had to be Ida, and the words he'd proudly used to describe her rang in Angel's ears: *Don't let the pretty face fool you. She runs the estate like a drill sergeant. I couldn't manage without her.*

Ida's shoes clacked authoritatively on the hardwood floor as she approached, arms outstretched toward her brother. They hugged warmly.

"It's good to have you back home, Everett."

"It's good to see you. Everything going well?"

Ida nodded. "And you? Get much work done while you were away?"

"I tried." Everett smiled. "Considering I had more than the usual distractions." He glanced toward Angel, who started to lift her hand in anticipation of a shake. Didn't happen. Feeling awkward, she quickly withdrew it.

"Virgil is around here somewhere," Ida said. "He wants to discuss some things with you."

Virgil was one of the business partners who had attended the wedding the day before. He and Everett spoke almost daily.

Everett nodded. "That can wait."

"How was being back on the island?" Ida asked. "You haven't been there in years."

This caught Angel off guard. Ida surely knew that the last time Everett had been on the island was with his late wife. Why would Ida bring that up now, in front of his new bride? Angel thought she could not have felt more unwelcomed, more out of place, if she had two red horns sticking out of her head. But she was determined not to let her assumptions get the better of her just yet. Although Ida's chilliness toward Angel certainly felt intentional, maybe she was wrong. Maybe she was being too sensitive. Maybe Ida was having a momentary brain lapse.

"Very relaxing, but it quickly got lonely since I know few people there," Everett said. "Too much time to think and dredge up old memories."

"I can imagine," Ida said.

"That is, until I met this one." He turned again toward his wife. "This is Angel. Angel, my sister, Ida."

Ida looked at Angel for the first time, extended a few fingers. "Hello."

"Hello," Angel said, nodding. "Nice to meet you."

They shook, and an uncomfortable silence descended over the room as everyone stood around with tight smiles lining their faces. Angel fixed her eyes back on the winding staircase.

"Should I place the bags in your suite, sir?" Jackson finally asked as he reentered the room and somehow managed to gather four suitcases at once.

"Yes, that sounds fine," Everett said. "Guess I'll go find Virgil now."

"Anything I can get for you, ma'am?" Jackson asked, looking at Angel.

Angel shook her head quickly and smiled, surprised to be addressed.

Everett looked at his sister. "Ida, why don't you give Angel a tour of the place?"

Angel suddenly realized just how exhausted she felt after the past few hectic days. "Um, I can wait in our room until you get done, Everett. I don't mind."

"It could be a while. Virgil and I have a lot to catch up on."

"I'd be happy to show you around," Ida said with a stiff smile on her face.

Angel turned to face Ida. Really? she thought, trying to shake off an eerie vision of her sister-in-law dragging her off by the hair and locking her in a cellar somewhere. Stop being silly, she told herself. Everett had said it took Ida a while to warm up to new people. "Thank you," Angel said. "I'd appreciate that."

"I'll catch up with you two later." Everett kissed Angel on the cheek.

"Dinner is at eight instead of seven tonight," Ida said. "I arranged it a little later than usual to give you two more time to settle in."

"You know, I'm sure Angel is bone-tired." Everett looked at Angel, who nodded. "I know I am. Have our dinner served on the terrace outside our room. And get Jackson to light the gas stove out there. It's a little chilly for October."

That sounded just dandy, Angel thought. She *was* drop-dead exhausted, and dinner with Ida could definitely wait for another evening.

"Not a problem," Ida said. "Come," she added to Angel. "I'll take you to the suite, then show you around."

As Angel dropped her handbag on a table just inside the doorway of the primary bedroom suite, she noticed Jackson and a housekeeper she hadn't yet met already unpacking and putting away their things. Angel had anticipated an introduction to the housekeeper who was handling her personals, but none was forthcoming, as Ida was already headed back out the door. "We'll come back here once they're done in there," Ida whispered. In her old life it would have been considered rude not to introduce strangers to each other, even if one was the help. But this was her new life. Things were a lot different now.

On the main level, they saw the formal dining and living rooms, a solarium, and a library, as well as a spa, home theater, and wine cellar. Inlaid marble floors and limestone fireplaces, new terms she had just picked up, were in almost every room of the house.

"How many other bedrooms besides ours?" Angel asked.

"Four guest bedrooms, all en suite. Five bedrooms, eight baths altogether. That doesn't include the two-bedroom guest-house, also en suite. I live in the caretaker's cottage, a short walk from the main house."

Angel nodded but was pretty sure she looked confused, somewhat embarrassed that she wasn't sure exactly what *en suite* meant.

"You know. Each bedroom has its own private bath."

"Oh."

"I'll take you to the second floor now." Each of the impressive guest bedrooms was decorated in a different color, from blue to peach to green. Angel didn't see how you would ever get a guest to go home after staying in one of these fully decked-out spaces, with fluffy pillows and comforters it looked like you could get lost in.

"We'll walk up from here but there's a private elevator that goes directly from the breakfast room to your primary suite. I'll show you that later." As they reached the landing on the top level, Angel realized that the primary bedroom took up the entire floor. Ida pushed the double doors open and she finally got time to check out the room, with its wall of floor-to-ceiling windows. Angel parted the closed drapes to reveal views of an expansive rolling green lawn dotted with gardens. Off in the distance she could glimpse the Potomac River between trees now resplendent in their striking fall hues. It was stunning. She could have stood there for hours taking it all in.

In the room, there were two of everything: baths, walk-in closets, mirrored dressing rooms. The only thing shared was a huge four-poster bed that Angel was sure must be bigger than a normal king-size. There was also a large sitting area with built-in bookcases, a minibar, and a marble fireplace.

The downside to all this, Angel realized at the end of her tour, was the overall mood in the entire house. It was dark, dreary, and depressing. The feelings hit her slowly, then spiraled as she and Ida moved from room to room. Finally she figured out the reason. All throughout the house heavy drapes were drawn tightly and the lights seemed to be on dimmers. It felt like the walls were closing in. Like a household in permanent mourning. Angel wanted to ask why after all this time since Chloe's death but decided to save that for Everett. Although Ida's personality had lightened up somewhat, she still was not exactly what one would call cheerful and fuzzy. It felt as if she were just doing her job at her brother's request. Nothing more.

"So," Ida said, clasping her hands together in the doorway, "would you like some refreshments while you wait for Everett? I can have them brought up."

"That would be nice. I am a little hungry."

"Consider it done."

"Thank you. Um, I have a question."

"Yes?"

"There was this one room on the floor below, you know, where the guest rooms are, that we didn't go into."

Ida arched her thick brows. Her shoulders stiffened. "And?"

Clearly Angel had struck a nerve. Had she crossed a line? But that was ridiculous. This was her house. She had a right to know what was in that room and any other for that matter. Still, this was her first day at Riverwild and meeting her sister-in-law. On some level she figured it was probably best not to ruffle any feathers so soon. She cleared her throat as a familiar feeling welled up inside her. The one that meant curiosity was going to win out over prudence, even if that arched brow had warned that she should behave otherwise. "What is it used for? Is it another guest room?"

"No. That's Mrs. Bruce's room. We rarely go in there." Ida stated this tersely with a tightening of her lips.

Chills tingled up Angel's arms. Ida had just referred to Chloe in the present tense. As if she were still living and breathing at this very minute, despite the fact that it had been more than a year since her death. For some reason Ida seemed reluctant to let her late sister-in-law go, even to the point of acting like she was still there in the house. Everyone had their own timetable for grieving, yes, but this felt a bit much. Angel was tempted to remind Ida that *Mrs. Bruce* was standing right here in front of her. *I'm Mrs. Bruce.* But she had a feeling it would be better to keep her mouth shut for now and wait until she saw Everett.

* * *

During dinner and a much-needed bottle of red wine, shared between the two of them on the terrace outside their bedroom that evening, the conversation was light and pleasant. It had been a long, eventful few days of traveling from Europe, getting married, being introduced to Riverwild. Angel decided not to risk dampening Everett's sprits by bringing up the mystery bedroom and Ida's strange comments. That could wait. They needed a quiet, relaxing moment to just enjoy being newlyweds. The views of the Potomac and the stars twinkling above were the perfect backdrop.

They both picked up their glasses after the meal, and he took her hand and steered her back inside. Neither said a word as he placed the glasses on the nightstand, then slowly removed her robe and released the spaghetti straps on her nightgown. It glided to the floor, and he smothered her neck and shoulders with wet, tender kisses. Next thing she knew they were sinking down toward the cotton sheets. His breath came fast and heavy as his warm, bare body pressed tightly, almost desperately, against hers. There was an intensity in his movements that she had never felt from him before. As if the air in this house had permeated her husband's being in a strange way, unearthing something hot and wild that lay deep inside him. Though unsure where all this passion was coming from, she decided to simply enjoy this new man in her bed.

13

"Sorry I'm so late," Everett said, as he exited the elevator and slipped into the seat across from Angel at the breakfast table. He was dressed for work in a tan suit and dress shirt, sans necktie. "Didn't realize I was so tired." They were in the solarium on the main level, just off the breakfast room. Surrounded on three sides by floor-to-ceiling windows, it had obviously been designed to allow in an abundance of morning light. Except it was anything but bright and airy here, or anywhere else in this mansion, with all the heavy off-white drapes drawn so tightly. Angel felt weary herself and suspected the dark atmosphere had a lot to do with her fatigue.

She suppressed a yawn, still in her nightie and robe, and yearned to crawl back between the sheets for some more shuteye. She wasn't used to such pervading gloominess and suspected that it would begin to affect her mood. The first thing she normally did in the morning when she'd lived in her condo was pull apart the curtains. Weather permitting in spring and fall, on crisp, breezy days like this, she opened the windows to let fresh air in. Somehow it seemed that such gestures would be unwelcome here.

"Good morning," she said, forcing a smile, trying to summon up some cheerfulness. "You look very handsome."

"It's after nine. Why didn't you wake me?"

His snappiness took her off guard; the smile quickly fell from her lips as she lowered her coffee cup. His attitude made her feel as if she'd done something wrong when really she was trying to be helpful. It had been weeks since Everett had slept in.

"I didn't want to disturb you. Figured you deserve a day to sleep longer. You work so hard."

"True enough," he said, his voice a little more even-tempered. "Will Ida be joining us?"

"Probably not if she isn't already here. She's usually first in, first out for breakfast. She may have grabbed a bite earlier this morning. I know some repair work is being done on the lighting system at the tennis courts. Something to do with the wiring. She's probably looking into that."

Angel nodded. That was good to hear. She wouldn't have wanted their brief, testy exchange the previous day to have been the reason for her sister-in-law's absence.

Almost as soon as Everett sat, a chef entered with a plate of eggs Benedict and smoked salmon and placed it in front of him along with a glass of freshly squeezed tomato juice. Once he departed, Angel leaned across the expansive table, closer to Everett. One thing about living in this place that really irked her—the too-frequent lack of privacy. Servant eyes and ears were always coming and going. They had just spent their most ardent night ever, and it was fresh on her mind. "We did have a very long, sexy night together," she whispered. "Wouldn't blame you for feeling tired."

To her surprise, Everett seemed to blush. "I . . . I hope I wasn't too rough," he muttered so softly she had to lean even closer. "I may have gotten carried away."

Why was he apologizing for a night of passion? It was fiery, steamy, a little bit kinky. Everett had been filled with longing, almost insatiable. But he hadn't harmed her in any way. Their lovemaking had always been pleasurable, but last night they'd entered a whole new realm. And she had enjoyed every minute of it.

"Well, I mean, I've never seen you like that. But I liked . . ."

"I don't know what came over me," he said, interrupting absentmindedly as he dived into his eggs. "Not like me. Really."

Angel narrowed her eyes. He was making such a big deal out of it; she wondered if maybe it *was* like him. Or had been. With Chloe. And if he'd been holding back on her all this time.

"It won't happen again," he added before she could comment.

She slumped back in her chair and stared at him. His jaw was set tightly, his thick brows furrowed deeply. He had barely looked her way since sitting down. What was going on with him? This was not at all the response she'd expected from him this morning, especially after the closeness of the previous night.

"Is everything all right, Everett? I mean, at the office? In general?"

"You keep asking me that."

"You seem, I don't know. Much more on edge. And guarded."

"Just tired, I guess. Overworked."

She nodded slightly, unconvinced. She would let this go for now. Maybe it really was exhaustion. Lord knew he worked long and hard enough. And if it were something else, hopefully he would share it with her. "You'll let me know if there's anything at all bothering you. Or anything I can do to help, right? And for the record, I enjoyed last night. There's no need to apologize."

He glanced up at her, hesitated for a second. Then he nodded. "Understood."

"Good."

He went back to his breakfast.

"I want to ask you a question, Everett. You know I had the tour yesterday. With Ida."

He took a sip of juice. "Mm-hmm. How was that?"

"Fine, I guess. I mean, the house is amazing. And huge. I got lost trying to find this room this morning." She chuckled at the memory of having to ask Ella, one of the downstairs housekeepers, for directions as she vacuumed the library.

"I'm sure you'll get the hang of things in no time. What was the question you wanted to ask?"

He had missed her attempt to lighten the mood. Again.

"Oh. It's about one of the rooms on the second floor. It's the only bedroom Ida didn't show me. I felt like I was being warned to stay away when I mentioned that. She said it was Chloe's room."

"Yes?" he asked, looking at her, brows raised.

"She used the present tense." Angel shivered slightly at the memory.

He smiled with affection. "Well, yes, she does tend to refer to it that way."

"And you don't think that's, um, odd?"

He shrugged. "It's Ida. That's her way of coping. She and Chloe were very close."

"Always?"

"I seem to remember it took a while for the relationship to develop."

Then maybe there was hope yet for a friendship with Ida, Angel thought. Everyone had their own way of dealing with death. She would leave it alone for now. "Fair enough. What do you keep in there? Anything special?"

"I haven't been inside since shortly after she died. I assume her personal things are still there."

"Sounds like the two of you slept in separate bedrooms."

"We did. For the last few months anyway."

She tilted her head. "Do you mind if I ask why? Something happen?"

He clenched his jaw. She had come to realize he often did that when there was something he preferred to keep to himself. "Just . . . not getting along so well. She wanted her space. I needed mine. Things worked better that way."

"So, it was her idea to sleep apart?"

He exhaled impatiently. "Look, Angel, that's over now, done." He dabbed the corners of his mouth with his cloth napkin and tossed it onto the table, looking as if he were ready to jump up and flee. "Let's not dwell on the past. I prefer to focus on now and the future. On us."

Angel nodded, half smiling. She knew that his marriage to Chloe had hit some rocky patches. But she had no idea it had reached the point of them sleeping in separate rooms. It was becoming clearer every day that something had happened during their marriage, something he found difficult to discuss. At least with her. She had one final question and then she'd shut up before really getting on his nerves.

"Would you mind if I take a look around in there?"

"Ah, probably best not to do that."

"But why?"

"Why would you want to? What's it got to do with you?"

She shrugged. "Just curious. I've heard so much about her. Her style, her life, her marriage to you. How could I not be?"

He grimaced. "Chloe was human, just like everyone else. With plenty of faults as well as virtues. She put one leg into her pants at a time."

Angel was speechless; her jaw dropped. This did not sound like Everett. All she wanted was to look around the room. Why was he being so defensive?

"Look, honey," he said, his tone softening. "I seriously doubt Ida is ready for anything like this. She does not want that room disturbed by anyone, not even me."

"So I gathered. But it's *our* house, Ev. I should be able to go where I want and do what I want without needing permission from her."

"Ida has been managing things around here ever since Chloe died and doing a damn good job."

"But you have a new wife now," she said pointedly.

He paused, clearly not expecting that. "All in due time. You've only been here a day. Be patient." He stood. "Let's give her a little more time to come around. Chloe's death hit us all very hard."

"I hear you," she said, realizing this wasn't going anywhere. "You know, maybe it would help cheer everyone up if we brightened the rooms around here, opened some of the drapes."

He sighed. "Well, that I agree with. I've spoken to Ida about it more than once."

Angel was so glad to hear this. The furniture and artwork looked like shadows looming in the darkness, especially on the lower level where the gym and spa were. She stood, strode to one of the windows in the solarium, and pulled on the drawstring. The drapes parted; sunlight flooded the space, immediately lifting her spirits.

"There. Isn't that a thousand percent better?" Without waiting for Everett's response, she moved around the room, opening the others to expose a huge garden outside filled with plants and shrubbery. A young man in a wide-brimmed hat trimmed the hedges. Off in the distance she could spot the wild waters of the Potomac River.

"Oh, look at this."

"It is beautiful, isn't it?" he said.

"I'll do this around the rest of the house."

"Whoa. Wait. I wouldn't go that far. Let me speak to Ida first."

Angel's shoulders dropped. There it was again. Ida, Ida,

Ida. It was strange to see this powerful man defer so much to his sister. "Oh, Everett, is that really necessary?"

"If she approves, we'll get one of the housekeepers to do it. That's a lot of rooms."

"Fine," she said tersely, folding her arms, not trying to hide her disappointment.

"Like I said, be patient." Everett grabbed his briefcase. "All in due time."

"Will you be home in time for dinner? Ida said it's at seven."

"I'll try my best."

"Do more than try, Everett." She dreaded the prospect of dining alone with Ida. "And what about the wedding reception? When are we going to start planning that?"

"Speak to Ida about it. She's very good at that kind of thing. Right up her alley."

Angel sighed with exasperation as he dashed off. Just what she wanted to hear. *Not.*

"Wait, aren't you forgetting something?" she called after him. She meant her goodbye kiss, but he had already vanished.

* * *

After finishing her omelette, Angel had an extra cup of coffee to steel her nerves for the talk with Ida that lay ahead. Then she changed into jeans and went off in search of her sister-in-law, who had mentioned that she could usually be found in her office next to the kitchen or in her cottage directly out the back door and down the path. Ida had said she preferred to be summoned by text or the wireless intercom system hooked up throughout the house and grounds. But Angel wanted an excuse to familiarize herself with the maze of hallways, rooms, and buildings that made up the estate.

She wandered around and soon found herself standing at the

entrance to the kitchen. She was about to continue on when the familiar scent of freshly baked bread drifted out to the hallway. She peeked inside to see gleaming top-of-the-line appliances in a kitchen almost the size of the commercial kitchen where she'd once worked. She stared for a few minutes, taking in the familiar sights, and imagined herself checking dishes before they went out for service. As her eyes roamed, she was reminded of being back in the kitchen in DC, collaborating with the head chef, supervising the staff—Alex, Elijah, Felix, and Diane—ordering food, and designing and testing menus. It had been hard work and not a luxurious lifestyle by any means; she didn't miss it as much as she did the feelings of confidence and competence it had inspired within her. Feelings that she sometimes missed these days.

She sighed wistfully and moved on to a small adjacent office, which she assumed was Ida's. The narrow room was empty save for a desk and a few file cabinets, so she walked out the back door and down a cobblestone footpath until she reached a one-story cottage surrounded by a small well-tended garden. She knocked softly and opened the door when she heard Ida's voice.

"Come on in. I'll be right there."

Angel stepped into a neatly furnished front room every bit as light deprived as the mansion. Dark, heavy drapes covered the lone window. She was trying to decide whether to sit on the couch just as Ida emerged from a back room, dressed smartly as usual in a stylish pair of slacks, sweater, and her ever-present pearl necklace. She was obviously surprised to see Angel there.

"Good morning. And what can I do for you?" Ida asked, her voice sounding concerned. She switched on a floor lamp; it cast a faint glow across Ida's furrowed brows. "Is there a problem?"

Angel paused, surprised for a moment by Ida's solicitousness. Then it hit her that it felt phony, but she decided to ignore it, knowing that Ida would love nothing better than to ruffle her feathers. "Hello, Ida. Everything is fine. Mind if we chat for a few minutes?"

"Well, I am in the middle of something, but yes, come on back."

Angel followed Ida into her office, lit by another floor lamp, and a glimmer coming from a laptop on the desk. This room was sparsely decorated with the bare necessities for an office space—one tall file cabinet, one waist-high bookcase. No wall hangings, no accessories. The only photo Angel noticed as she slid down into the chair facing Ida was a brass-framed picture of Ida with Everett and Chloe sitting on the desk. It had been taken at what appeared to be a New Year's Eve celebration from three years past, judging from the date on the decorations. Angel sat and searched for a place to park her hands, finally resting them prayerfully in her lap. Would she ever feel at ease around this woman?

"Cozy place you have here, Ida."

"Thank you."

"How have you been?"

"I'm fine," Ida said, sitting up straight in her chair, eyeing Angel in a way that made her feel like an invader from another world. "Tell me what brings you here."

So much for small talk, Angel thought. Clearly not Ida's forte. No surprise there. Angel cleared her throat and racked her brain for the words she had practiced on the walk down the hill but now seemed to have vacated her memory. She was drawing a complete blank as Ida stared sharply, fingernails tapping her desk, brows furrowed with impatience.

"Um, Everett and I, well, he said I should talk to you about planning our wedding reception."

Ida now lifted one of those brows. "A wedding reception? He didn't mention anything about a reception to me."

He didn't need to, Angel thought. Because *she* was mentioning it to her now. But she didn't dare say that.

"*We* discussed it," Angel said. "Since we had a small, quick wedding, we want to throw a big party. You know, something lively, fun, fancy."

"Oh? And just where and when did you have in mind?"

"I was thinking here, in the early spring. That should give us plenty of time to plan."

Ida scoffed. "That's not nearly enough time. Impossible."

"That's almost six months."

"You need at least a year to plan a large gathering if done right. I've done it on the estate many times."

Angel found it hard to believe that anything festive ever happened around here these days. Which was precisely why they needed to throw a big bash. Liven things up. "When do you suggest, then?"

"I can't tell you that this minute," Ida said with a shrug. "I'll have to give it some thought."

"Mm-hmm." Obviously, Ida was not going to make this easy. Or pleasant. Angel squeezed her fingers, reminded herself that *she* was now Mrs. Bruce. "Fine. I'll have my husband speak to you."

Ida glared at Angel for a few silent seconds. Angel found it difficult to read Ida's expression, to determine whether her passive little threat would have any impact at all. Finally, Ida picked up the tablet sitting next to her laptop. "We might be able to make next summer work. July, August," she said, without looking up.

"It will be so hot by then. There's no way to have it sooner?"

Ida smirked. "We don't throw get-togethers here. You can't possibly plan something worthy of Riverwild quickly. Trust me. Before Chloe asked me to come and work at the mansion, shortly after they were married, I owned an event-planning business. I know what I'm talking about, Angel. July at the earliest."

Angel hated the thought of waiting so long and even more of

having Ida dictate things to her. She could hire someone else but that would just invite trouble. She was brand-new to Riverwild. It would be foolish to try and plan her first big affair without Ida's help. "Fine. July then."

"Good." Ida stood. "I'll check with Everett and make sure to pick a date in July that will work for him."

Angel cleared her throat, stood up. "*I'll* speak to my husband and get back to you."

They stared each other down for a moment, as if facing off before coming to blows. Ida finally blinked, nodded ever so slightly, like she had suddenly remembered that her brother had a wife. And that said wife was right there in front of her. "Of course. But the sooner I can get it on the books, the better."

Yeah, yeah, Angel thought, relieved that she'd held her ground, at least on having the event. She would have preferred not needing to invoke her husband's name to get Ida to take her seriously. For a fleeting second she thought of mentioning the drapery up at the mansion but quickly brushed that aside. Right now, all she wanted was to get the heck out of there and retreat to her bedroom, where she had some control of her environment. It wasn't much, considering she was supposed to be the mistress of Riverwild. But it was the only place where she felt any comfort whenever Everett wasn't around.

She hit the path back to the house and made a beeline up to the primary bedroom sitting area. She slipped down into one of the two armchairs facing the fireplace and hugged a pillow. The swath of sunlight coming from a side window, so rare around here, felt like a warm embrace. Exactly what she needed after that encounter with Ida. She could not understand the coldness coming from her sister-in-law. Why? Whatever for? Did Ida think she was not good enough for her brother? Or that she wasn't cultured or rich enough to carry the Bruce name?

This would not be the first time someone from "society" had

seemed to think that way. Angel had learned not to allow the snobbery and slights from people who looked down on her to get to her. But this wasn't just any other person. This was the family she had married into. She was going to have to figure out how to turn things around with Ida or live her life in misery. Or . . . Angel didn't want to let her mind even approach the third alternative. The *D* alternative. She and Everett were just getting started. But she could never spend the rest of her life living under a roof with someone who seemed to want to knock her down at every turn.

She thought of bringing this problem to Everett's attention in hopes that he would insist Ida be more considerate of his wife's needs and opinions. After breakfast this morning, though, she was convinced that would be a waste of time. Hopefully she could get him to understand someday. For now, he seemed beholden to his sister, with one excuse after another for her rude behavior. Her husband should have her back on these things, but she was all on her own.

14

The bouncing on the other side wouldn't quit. It was relentless. Each time Angel finally dozed off, the bed rocked again, plunging up and down, as if on angry seas. Angel would struggle groggily in the darkness, shifting from one side to the other, until, at last, she felt herself slowly drift back to sleep.

And then it hit again. This time she sensed something different—a heavy thump, a light breeze. She shuddered, slid closer to where her husband lay, wanting to feel the safety of his warm body. But all she felt was a cold, empty space. She sat up quickly, flipped on the bedside lamp. Everett had vanished, the covers tossed back in a heap.

She swung her feet to the floor, threw on a robe, walked all around the suite: the sitting area, his-and-her bathrooms, walk-in closets. He was nowhere to be found. In the few weeks she'd lived at Riverwild, he'd had more and more trouble sleeping. Sometimes she woke up to find him staring at the ceiling in the darkness, arms folded tightly across his chest. And always, whenever she asked if he was okay, his answer was the same.

"I'm fine. Go back to sleep."

This was the first time she had awoken to find his side of the bed empty. She threw the door open and walked down one level. She dashed up the hallway, checking each guest room, one after the other. She swung the door at the farthest end and noticed a figure lying on its back. Squinting through the blackness, she walked cautiously toward the bed.

"Everett?"

"Huh?" He jumped at her voice, lifted his head. His eyes darted around the room, seeming dazed, lost.

"Everett," she repeated, standing next to the bed. "Are you all right?"

He leaned up on one elbow, gazed at her blankly, blinking rapidly. "Chloe?"

She froze. A sharp pang ran across her chest. His voice was hoarse, anxious. She couldn't believe what she'd just heard, and her instinct was to lash out. But he looked so confused, so help-less. Now was not the time to get upset. She took a deep breath. "It's me, honey. Angel."

He frowned. "I'm . . . I don't . . ." He shook his head as if try-ing to clear it.

She sat on the edge of the bed next to him, reached out, pulled him into her arms, sensing that what he needed now was to be comforted. She feared she'd startled him from a deep slumber, or maybe a bad dream. "Shh," she said, cradling him softly. He allowed her to soothe him for a few minutes.

She switched on the nightstand lamp, and when she peered into his face again, he seemed his old self. Groggy yet earthbound.

But what was he doing in the guest room? "Were you having a nightmare?" she asked.

He nodded slowly, touched his forehead. "I think so."

She glanced around. "Why are you in here?"

"Couldn't sleep. Got up and walked around the house, then

came in here and watched TV until I felt drowsy. Didn't want to disturb you, so I decided to sleep here instead."

"You've been having trouble since we got here. On the island you used to sleep like a rock."

"I know."

"It feels weird for you to be in here. Come on back to our room." She tugged him by the arm, but he pulled away.

"What's wrong?"

"Nothing. But I'll just keep you awake tossing and turning if I go back."

"Ev."

"Yes?"

"You called out her name."

He looked at her sharply. "Whose name?"

"Chloe's. When I walked up to the bed, you called me Chloe."

He frowned, shook his head. "I . . I thought I had licked this problem on vacation. I guess not. It's this damn house. It's all coming back."

A wave of alarm ran through her gut. Her heart picked up a beat. This did not seem like Everett. She peered into his eyes. He was alert now but they still seemed off, darting to and fro, avoiding her gaze. "Everett you're starting to spook me. What's coming back?"

"The insomnia," he whispered, massaging his forehead.

"I didn't know you had insomnia."

He nodded. "Yeah, it can get bad. I have got to get control of this thing."

What the heck did that mean? He spoke as if the insomnia or whatever was bothering him were a living, breathing entity, chasing him around. She looked about again. This was the largest of the guest bedrooms and had the most masculine decor, with dark wood furniture and bedding. Suddenly something dawned on her. "Was this once your room?"

He hesitated, then nodded. "We both had our own rooms to get away to whenever we needed some time apart."

"I see." She stood, folded her arms firmly. "Well, we're not going to do this."

"Do what?"

"Sleep apart. I don't like it."

"It's not permanent, but for now it's best."

"I don't agree."

"I'll call my sleep doctor first thing in the morning," he said with finality. "Haven't seen him in a while."

"Sleep doctor?" She'd had no idea there was even such a thing.

"He helped me out a lot when I found out that Chloe . . ." He stopped abruptly. She could tell that he had just blurted out more than he'd intended.

"When you found out what, Everett?"

He clammed up as he often did when the discussion turned to his deceased wife.

"Talk to me, Everett. Please! We've only been at Riverwild a few weeks and already you're deserting me. I need an explanation."

"Stop exaggerating. I'm not deserting you."

"That's what it feels like. I didn't get married to sleep alone."

He let out a deep gust of air. "The truth is, and I guess you should know this . . ."

"Go on."

"The last year or so of our marriage was rough, worse than I've let on. We grew apart, but decided to try and work it out. Things got a little better for a while and she got pregnant. It wasn't planned yet I couldn't have been happier. She was not exactly thrilled about it but seemed to be coming around. Then she had a miscarriage."

"Oh, I'm so sorry to hear that."

"I wanted to try again as soon as she recovered but . . ."

Angel watched as his expression quickly changed from one of deep sorrow to unbridled bitterness.

"She absolutely refused," he continued through tight teeth. "I practically begged, and when I kept pushing, she . . . she confessed. Said the baby wasn't even mine."

"What?"

He jumped up, paced the floor, clenched his fists. "She admitted it was someone else's kid. She had been having an affair the entire time we were supposed to be fixing our marriage."

"Good grief," Angel said. This was the last thing she'd expected. "Was she in love with the guy?"

"It was Reggie."

"Who?"

"Reggie Hawthorne. The artist you met at the gallery in Edgartown."

Angel was silent for a second, trying to absorb what she'd just heard. Then she gasped, covered her mouth with her hand.

"I believe they met when we visited the island shortly after our marriage and kept in touch without my knowledge. His family has a house there and he goes every year from May to August. I always wondered why she never wanted to go back with me after that summer." He sneered. "She preferred being with her young lover."

Angel closed her eyes. "Now I get why you were so angry when you saw him."

"The one condition I gave Jackie when I funded the summer exhibits was *not* to allow him to display his work there. I didn't tell her why, so she had no idea of the seriousness of my objections. Still, seeing him there pissed me off."

Now Angel understood completely why he had gotten so hot under the collar when they unexpectedly ran into Reggie. And why he was so reluctant to talk about his late wife. Everyone who had ever mentioned her seemed to think she'd walked on water, that their marriage was to be envied. The truth was anything but.

"Why didn't you say something sooner, Ev? I mean, I get

why not at first. This is horrible. But we're married now. We shouldn't have secrets like this."

"It's hard to talk about. People think we were this glamorous, perfect power couple." He scoffed. "If they knew the truth, they'd be shocked."

"True. I know I am."

"Despite all her alluring qualities—the beauty, charisma, impeccable social skills—Chloe could be incredibly self-absorbed. Always wanting what she wanted when she wanted it with little consideration for how it might affect anyone else. This house was all her doing. She had to have the biggest, most luxurious place in all of Potomac. She could be a total bitch, thinking only of herself. Sorry, but that's how I feel."

It was like a dam had burst, Angel thought, shaking her head at the revelations coming forth. At least he had finally opened up to her.

"Do you think maybe that's why she took her life?"

He stopped pacing the floor. "What?"

"Losing the baby. The affair. And then admitting it all to you. That had to have been emotionally draining for her."

"Could be. She was really down on herself toward the end. Said she hated her life. But she was a complicated woman, and it's always hard for those of us left behind to understand why someone would do that."

Angel nodded. Her aunt on her mother's side had committed suicide when Angel was a child. No one really ever understood why. Lots of speculation but no clarity; her aunt took her reasons to the grave with her.

"Look, what I just told you about Reggie and the baby must always stay between just us. It would kill her parents and many others if they knew the truth. Not even Ida knows about this."

"I understand. You know you can trust me."

He took her hands into his. "I believe that. I think I've felt it from the beginning. And I promise that sleeping in here will only be temporary. A couple of nights tops. Just need to talk to my doctor. Until then, there's no point in neither of us getting a decent night's rest."

He pulled her toward him, kissed her lips. She tried to smile, to show strength and support. She hated this, but he was finally starting to trust her and she wanted to respect his wishes. She walked back to the primary bedroom and slipped beneath the covers, where she lay awake for the rest of the night.

* * *

Angel soon began to realize that Everett's promise meant nothing. And if sleeping by herself for a week in a huge bed in a strange house was not torture enough, three days of violent thunderstorms up and down the East Coast were thrown into the mix. She spent night after night all alone while thunder clapped in the distance and rain pelted the windows.

He even joined her at breakfast less often. Some mornings he didn't bother to sit, just planted a quick, dry peck on her forehead before dashing to the office. Ida had started to take breakfast in her cottage down the path as soon as Angel moved to Riverwild. Not that she minded Ida's absences first thing in the morning, but she realized that if things were ever going to get any better around here, she and Everett's sister had to at least get on cordial terms. That would never happen if they constantly avoided each other.

Many mornings she found herself staring at the silverware, studying the intricate design, wondering how much it had cost. Or thinking of taking up sketching again. But her heart just wasn't in it these days. Dinners were not much better. When the three of them showed up, they barely spoke, just quickly shoved down their food before retreating to their separate spaces at different corners of the estate.

What had she gotten herself into? And how? She stood up from the breakfast table, parted the drapes, and stared out onto the wet, slimy grounds. The slick lawn, the gloomy skies. This was nothing at all like the life she had anticipated with Everett. She'd married a powerful businessman. A billionaire. They were supposed to go dining and dancing together, take leisurely, luxurious vacations all around the globe, talk of starting a family. Instead, she now realized that she had wed a man who was deeply troubled by a dark and deceitful first marriage, a closed book who was pushing her away.

Sometimes when she looked closely into the face across the table, she barely recognized the man who sat there. He seemed preoccupied, and so unhappy. If she tried to reach out and comfort him, or asked what was troubling him, his reply, like a rehearsed speech, was always the same: "Fine. Busy. Working hard. Just need more time." The gloomy rooms of this house had swallowed the happy couple that met on Martha's Vineyard, and regurgitated two distant strangers. She was painfully disappointed and lonely yet felt powerless to turn things back to the way they'd once been.

Her only moments of solace came when chatting on the phone with Dawn and Patrice, two friends from her old life, a life she desperately missed. They gossiped, reminisced, laughed out loud. Dawn and Patrice got a big kick out of teasing her about becoming filthy rich.

"I can't even relate," Dawn had said one afternoon as they chatted for more than an hour, Angel sitting at her bedroom window overlooking the gardens below. "You're probably carrying Birkin bags and wearing Manolo Blahnik heels."

Angel didn't mention that a Birkin bag had been her first purchase on their visit to Paris, during an afternoon spent at Hermès, prearranged by one of Everett's assistants.

But beneath the giggles and gaiety, Dawn admitted that she was worried. She had detected something different in her friend's voice since she'd arrived at Riverwild. When Angel kept insisting that all was okay, Dawn tore herself away, despite being several months pregnant, and dragged Patrice along through the rain to pay Angel a visit. Angel was so excited to have this slice of her old life coming to Riverwild. As soon as Jackson, alerted by security at the front gate, mentioned that her guests had arrived, she ran to the front door and waited for the car to come up the half-mile-long driveway. She was thrilled to see their smiling faces alight from Patrice's tan Honda in their ripped jeans and leather boots.

In the vestibule, they hugged warmly, fussed over Dawn's protruding belly, and admired Angel's ginormous diamond ring. Her friends could barely contain their astonishment as Jackson led them down the wide halls of the mansion, past one elegantly decorated room after another, and into the solarium with its towering ceiling. The three of them huddled and caught up as Jackson served tea and sweets.

"OMG. This place is almost too much," Dawn said, one hand cradling her pregnant belly, the other picking out a pastry. "I would get lost in here."

"I know," Patrice said, fingering her dyed waist-length blond locks. "I'm scared to touch anything. You look different, too."

"Mm-hmm. More glam," Dawn said.

Angel squirmed in her seat, not wanting to mention the loneliness she felt creeping up on her each day, how isolated she had become. It felt silly to complain, to be anything but happy, with all that she now had. "I did get lost a few times the first week."

"How are you dealing with all the changes in your life?" Dawn asked.

Angel shrugged, looked down at the floor. "One day at a time, but I'm fine." She looked back up. "I mean, these are good problems to have, right?"

Dawn narrowed her eyes with doubt. "Uh-huh. We've known each other since grade school, Angel. You don't seem fine to me."

"I can see it, too," Patrice said. "You're more, I don't know, subdued. It feels like you're holding back."

Angel sighed. "It's been a difficult adjustment. I won't lie."

"I don't doubt that," Dawn said.

"Does that seem selfish?" Angel asked. "To have all this and not be satisfied?"

"Trying to manage a big-ass house like this would challenge anybody," Patrice said.

"It's not even about that," Angel said. "We have an estate manager who takes care of everything. And Jackson, the man who answered the door, helps. I wish I *did* have some say in how things get done around here."

"You mean you don't?" Dawn asked.

Angel shook her head. "I can barely open the drapes without feeling like I need permission."

"What?" they both said in unison, mouths open.

"I kid you not."

"I assumed they were closed because of all the rain we've been having lately," Patrice said.

"So it's always this dark in here?" Dawn asked, glancing around.

Angel nodded. "In every room. Sun, rain, day, night. Boss's orders."

"By boss, you mean Everett?" Dawn asked.

"Oh, no. His sister, Ida."

Dawn and Patrice stared at each other. Patrice shuddered with exaggeration. "Weird."

"Did you talk to Everett about it?" Dawn asked. "He needs to remind his sister that you're the mistress of the household now. *You* should be the boss."

"I tried. But Ida has been running the show for a while now, ever since his first wife died. Everett agrees with whatever she says."

"This is Everett Bruce we're talking about?" Patrice said, pretending to need clarity.

Angel nodded. "I know. Hard to imagine, isn't it? Neither of them seems ready to change a darn thing around here. I'm beginning to find it easier to just go along."

"That does not sound like you, Angel," Dawn said.

"Nope," Patrice said. "Not at all. You commanded an entire kitchen staff at Georgia's, for God's sake."

"Tell me about it. But he's so reluctant to go against his sister's wishes. It's like it's two against one. I can't explain it." She threw up her hands.

"Is his sister married?" Dawn asked. "Does she have children?"

Angel shook her head. "Nope. She lives here on the estate. In a small house just down the road.

"I think I saw it when we drove up," Dawn said. "What's she like?"

"Smart, fashionable, always . . ."

"That's not what I mean," Dawn said, interrupting. "Personality-wise."

Angel pressed her lips tightly and zipped them with her fingers.

"The wicked witch of Riverwild," Patrice said jokingly.

Angel's eyes widened. "Your words, not mine."

Dawn smiled with empathy. "Anything we can do? Maybe the three of us should have a chat with her."

"Yeah," Patrice said. "Sister-in-law needs a little talking to."

Angel couldn't help but smile as visions of her two friends from DC confronting Ida flashed by. "Thanks, ladies, but no thanks. I have to live here after you two leave, you know." But she was beginning to feel more like her old self after spending an afternoon hanging with her friends.

15

The visit from Dawn and Patrice a week earlier had done Angel a world of good, reminding her of the woman she had once been, and not all that long ago. Confident, commanding, contented. It hadn't been a perfect life by any means. Work hours were long and tough. Keeping up with her bills had been a real struggle. And her dating life had been a challenge, with long, lonely stretches between boyfriends who cheated or otherwise turned out to be big disappointments.

Yet she'd been nothing like the tentative, insecure, doubtful person lately strolling warily through the halls of Riverwild. She had completely lost her moxie, could see that clearly after spending time with her friends. How had she allowed her self-esteem to sink so low? And why? She had to fix this one way or another; she could not go on living like this.

Following a quick breakfast of coffee, juice, and toast, she slipped into a fleece jacket and rubber boots and headed out the back door. The woodsy property was muddy from all the recent rain, and she had to weave her way among the puddles littering the lawn. But the trees, now nearly bare, were breathtaking in their raw beauty and a stunning contrast against the sky. They made up for all the damp dreariness—both outdoors and in the dark halls of the house.

She passed quickly by the guesthouse and pool, then strolled slowly through the herb garden where the invigorating scent of mint growing in containers filled the air. She nodded at Ethan, the newly hired gardener, and his small crew as they carefully tended the rosemary and sage plants. Finally, she reached a clearing at the top of a hillside and paused to look down at the swirling waters of the four-hundred-mile-long Potomac River below. This had become her favorite spot on the estate, far away from the claustrophobic confines of the depressing rooms in the house and the hostile looks from her sister-in-law. She'd spent countless hours standing and gazing absentmindedly while taking in the glorious wonders of nature surrounding her.

Today's visit, though, had a more intentional purpose. She shoved her hands into the pockets of her jacket to ward off a chilly breeze as her mind wandered back to the visit from her friends. They brought back memories of her days working as the sous-chef at Georgia's, and as a private chef in DC and on Martha's Vineyard. She closed her eyes and tried to summon the strength she'd felt back then as a supervisor with employees and clients who depended on her. Even crabby Mrs. Harrison, who seemed to relish nothing more than giving her a hard time, had hired her year after year to cook for her family. She must have been doing something right.

Somehow, in barely a couple of months here, she'd lost all that. She had allowed outside forces to take over her life. It felt as if she were constantly under the watchful eyes of her husband's late wife through his sister and could barely make a move otherwise. Her husband continued to allow it to happen for reasons she could not figure out. Being married naturally entailed change and compromise but shouldn't mean completely losing herself. Even when married to a man like Everett Bruce.

She took a deep breath, released it slowly. Then she headed back toward the house with a newfound determination to claim her rights as Mrs. Bruce. She would start with those stupid drapes and wouldn't bother to ask permission from anyone. Why should she? It was *her* house. After handing her coat and boots to Jackson, she dashed from room to room on the main level until she found Ella, one of the downstairs maids, dusting the mantel in the library. Everett had been absolutely right: the drapes were bulky and heavy and there were a ton of them. She needed help.

Ella hesitated at first. Angel could see the alarm gathering in her eyes.

"But Miss Bruce insists they stay closed at all times, ma'am," Ella said.

Angel squared her shoulders, looked closely at Ella. "Well, I'm *Mrs.* Bruce. And I've decided I want them opened during the day from now on. Clear?"

Ella nodded slowly in compliance. "Of course, Mrs. Bruce."

Angel and Ella spent the next hour going from room to room on the two lower levels, pushing buttons and pulling on cords to reveal the outdoor scenery surrounding them. Then they hit the guest room level, stopping only when they reached the closed door to Chloe's bedroom. Ella froze, wringing her hands. Before Angel could try to put her at ease, the door opened and Ida stepped out, quickly shutting the door behind her.

It was the first time Angel had gotten so much as a glimpse inside that room, having tried the doorknob a few times only to find it locked. She'd just caught sight of a plush ivory-colored carpet and a fireplace. The fresh scent of lemon breezed by. The way Ida blocked the entrance you'd think she were standing guard at Fort Knox.

Angel had prepared mentally for this moment, or tried to, knowing that Ida would be around the house somewhere as she and Ella went about their task. She hadn't anticipated they would run into her directly outside this particular room.

Ida glanced quickly from Angel to Ella and back again. "What is going on here?"

Ella instinctively stepped back.

Angel was determined to hold her ground. "We're opening all the blinds and drapes," she said, hoping she sounded more authoritative than she felt. Her earlier courage was starting to dwindle in the presence of her sister-in-law.

"Excuse me?" Ida asked in a tone that dared Angel to repeat her words.

Angel cleared her throat. "I just said . . ."

"I heard what you said. Does Everett know about this?"

"I . . . Well, no. I'll explain it to him as soon as he gets back from his business trip tonight. I'm sure he'll be fine with it. He told me he has wanted this for a while."

Ida glared with contempt, her gaze traveling slowly from Angel to a clearly panicked Ella. "You should know better than this," Ida said.

"She was only doing as I asked," Angel said before Ella could speak. Angel turned to Ella. "You can go now."

As Ella eagerly flew down the hallway, Angel turned back toward Ida, who looked like she was about to have a stroke.

"What the hell do you think you're doing, Angel? I was talking to her."

"We need to let some light into this gloomy place, Ida. It's depressing to have . . ."

"It's too soon."

"It's been more than a year. Look, I know the two of you were very close but . . ."

"You would *never* understand, so don't pretend to," Ida hissed, her fists clenched at her sides. "You know nothing about Chloe. Or Riverwild. She had a remarkable eye. She decorated this house from the ground up. She chose every piece of furniture, every painting, every carpet." Ida paused to catch her breath. "Her spirit lives in each of these rooms, especially this one. You will never replace her, no matter how hard you try. *Never.*"

Now Angel had to take a step back to avoid the spittle spewing from Ida's mouth. She was stunned speechless. She had anticipated resistance from her sister-in-law but nothing like this over-the-top outburst. Being fond of someone was one thing, but this was way beyond that. This felt like obsession. It was odd to realize that a woman as formidable as Ida had such a huge, gaping weakness.

Ida stood silently, arms now folded tightly across her chest. Angel decided she had done enough to brighten up the place for one day. Let Ida have dominion over her precious late mistress's room. Angel would stop for now but was in no way defeated. This just left her more resolved not to back down entirely.

"I have one question," Angel said.

Ida glared scornfully, the veins popping at her temples.

Angel cleared her throat. "Who plans the menus? The chef?"

"*I* do. We both do."

"I want to be involved with that from now on."

Ida lifted her brow. "Oh, now Angel," she said, clearly struggling to control her voice. "That really is not necessary. I plan them weekly with the head chef, then Everett approves. This has worked smoothly for us for more than a year now."

"Yes, but . . ."

"Haven't you been pleased with the meals?" Ida asked with a sweetness every bit as fake as her smile.

"They have been delicious, Ida. Olivia is an excellent chef. That's not the point."

"Well, then, what . . ."

"Tell me, how did it work when Chloe was alive?"

"Excuse me?"

"When Chloe was here, did you plan the meals with the chef?"

Ida blinked. "Yes. Well, I mean, no. Chloe handled it. But she had an excellent palate. She dined in the finest restaurants all over the world. She had a flair for these things."

Angel may not have dined all over the world, but she was no slouch when it came to knowing how to prepare a menu and a good meal. "I'm not sure whether you're aware, but I worked for several years as a sous-chef at a top restaurant in DC, and also as a private chef for some of the finest families around."

Ida swallowed hard. "I . . . I had no idea. Everett never mentioned anything about that. He simply said he met you on Martha's Vineyard."

"I'm pretty sure I can handle a menu for three people."

Ida hesitated, and Angel could see the wheels turning in her head. Finally, Ida exhaled. "Very well . . . I'll explain that to Olivia."

"I can do that myself."

Ida nodded stiffly. "Of course."

Angel turned and walked down the hallway as Ida stood frozen to her spot outside Chloe's room.

As soon as Everett arrived home that evening, Angel took care to explain the changes that were happening around River-wild as they chatted in the sitting area of their bedroom suite before dinner.

"I noticed the windows as soon as I walked in," he said, loosening his necktie. "And she was okay with that?"

"You mean Ida?" Angel leaned back in her chair. "Oh, she's fine with it." Angel didn't think it necessary to bother him with the details. "How do *you* like it?"

"I . . . I think it looks great. I had forgotten how stunning everything looks from inside when it's opened up like this, even after dark, with the outdoor lights around the property, the moon in the distance."

"Good. I'm glad that you like it. I had the chef prepare meat loaf, mashed potatoes, and kale for dinner, just the way you like it. Picked out a bottle of your favorite cabernet sauvignon from the wine cellar. It should all be ready in about twenty minutes."

"Really?" he said, sounding pleased. "Can't remember when I last had that."

"I fixed it for you on the island, remember?"

He smiled as the memory came back to him. "I do now."

"I'll be handling the menus from here on. Had a long talk with Olivia. I'm excited to get started with that."

He nodded. "Really? Um . . ." He paused.

"Yes?"

"How is Ida dealing with all these changes? She enjoyed preparing the menus."

"Ida will be fine." Or not, Angel thought to herself. It might take his sister a while to get used to the changes, but she'd eventually come around. She had no choice as far as Angel was concerned.

Everett eyed Angel more closely, as if sensing something new about her presence. "You seem different."

"Really? How so?"

"I'm not certain. Maybe more upbeat. More sure of yourself."

She smiled. "I'm getting there."

"What brought all this on? Anything in particular?"

Yes, she thought. A visit from two friends. A trip down memory lane to better, stronger days. And a long talk with herself. "Nothing special. It was just time."

"I see. Will Ida be eating with us tonight?"

"I have no idea."

"I'm not going to get chewed out by my sister anytime soon, am I, Angel?"

She looked at him with studied innocence. "Why on earth would she do that? We talked, came to an agreement. Everything is fine. You can stop worrying." She stood up. "Now, I'm heading down to check on things. Can I have Jackson fix you a cocktail while you change?"

Ida did not grace them with her presence at dinner; she remained out of sight the rest of the evening.

But that was just as well. Angel and Everett chatted nonstop, enjoying each other's company like it was old times back on the island. He seemed to sense a fresh attitude in his wife, even joked that her mood felt contagious. She hadn't seen him smile as much since they'd first arrived at Riverwild. This house had tied him up in knots, just as it had dampened her spirits. Things were finally turning around, and it was good to spend time with the Everett she had fallen in love with.

After they had polished off a delicious old-fashioned peach cobbler for dessert, he lifted his glass of champagne to toast. "Here's to comfort food and my beautiful, radiant wife. I love you."

"I love you, too."

The following hours were some of the most romantic they had shared in weeks, with just the right combination of sweetness and passion and some of their best lovemaking ever.

Which was why she was puzzled when he suddenly hopped up in the middle of the night just as she was dozing off, slipped into his silken pajamas, and strolled to the doorway. When she asked him why he insisted on sleeping elsewhere, he responded simply, "So that I *can* sleep. It's impossible for anyone who hasn't experienced insomnia to understand how miserable it makes you feel."

"So explain it to me," she said, sitting up in the bed. "How *does* it make you feel?"

He paused at the door. "Sluggish, unmotivated. I have to force myself to get things done."

"I do sense that some days, but I assumed it was from being back here."

He shrugged. "It's both. Being back here has triggered a lot of bad memories."

"Is that it? Or is there something more?"

He lifted his brows. "Meaning?"

"The affair with Reggie and the baby and all that . . ." She paused. He seemed to be having such a difficult time letting the past go, she was beginning to wonder if he still had feelings for his late wife.

"Yes?"

"It was terrible, but life involves dealing with hard things all the time. And we go on. You're such a strong, confident man normally. Yet it's been so hard for you to get past that. Why? Is there something you're not telling me?"

"What are you implying?"

She noticed he was clenching his fists at his side. "I'm just asking if . . ."

"What happened was damn sure no small thing," he said with his practiced patience. "I hope you understand that."

"Of course. I'm not saying it was insignificant in any way. What I'm trying to . . ." She paused, searching for the right words. But there really were no right words for a wife to ask her husband if he still had feelings for his late wife. "Do you think that maybe you still carry some feelings for her?" There. She'd finally gotten it out.

He lifted his brows "For Chloe? C'mon. Hell no. Not at all. I'm past that."

She nodded, not so sure herself. This whole household seemed obsessed with Chloe.

"Look. It wasn't just that one thing between us," he said, as if sensing her skepticism. "Even before the affair, we had grown apart."

"Yes, but . . ."

"We argued a lot. All the damn time. She grew increasingly unhappy. With me, with the marriage. And when Chloe was not happy, she could be harsh. Mean at times. She was an only child, spoiled, and used to getting her way. I tried so hard but . . ." He shook his head, and she could see that this was extremely difficult for him to talk about, but she wanted him to keep going. The more he shared about that time in his life, the better she would understand this complicated man and his relationship with Chloe.

"Go on," she said anxiously, fearing that she was about to lose him. That he was about to close up and shut her out. Again. "You said she could be mean. How so?"

He shook his head as if to clear it, tightened his lips. "Look. It's late and I have work tomorrow."

"Everett, please . . ."

He blew her a kiss. "We'll talk more another time." Then he was gone.

She fell back onto the pillows, closed her eyes. But would they? Would he ever really open up about that painful period in his life? Or would he continue to keep her in the dark?

16

The pangs of loneliness at Riverwild still stabbed at her almost daily. True, her bond with her new husband had blossomed over the past several months. Many of their moments together were passionate, tender, loving. But there were far too few of them. Although he was letting her in more, she still felt she was being held at a distance. He continued to work hours on end, often arriving home well after dinnertime. Then he fell asleep, exhausted from the day's work, in his separate bed, in his separate bedroom. His business trips had picked up to once or twice monthly, leaving her alone in the big house for days at a time.

His bad dreams happened more frequently, almost nightly. Once, she got up around 2:00 a.m. and wandered to the kitchen for an ice-cold glass of water, her throat feeling parched from a slight head cold. As she approached the staircase, a sound spilled out into the hallway from Everett's room—a long, low wail, almost a cry. She turned and entered to find him in bed, twisting and tossing in obvious agony between sheets soaked with his sweat. When she shook him awake, he stared at her blankly for several minutes, perspiration dripping down his face. She had the linen changed and soothed him until he finally dozed off twenty minutes later, then made her way back to her own bed, her brows furrowed deeply in thought. The glass of water had been all but forgotten in the face of her husband's increasingly fragile state of mind.

Her relationship with Ida remained as strained as ever. Although they were cordial with each other whenever necessary, Angel could sense resentment oozing from her pores. Sometimes Ida avoided her entirely. Like the evening she'd caught a glimpse of her sister-in-law at the opposite end of a first-floor hallway, only to see her dart into a side room before they crossed paths.

As for her girlfriends, their last meeting had been at a farewell party thrown by her former boss at Georgia's around the first of the year. The outing had been a warm, fun walk down memory lane, a gathering of old friends and former co-workers filled with lots of smiles and laughter. Something she'd much needed. She had found herself dreading the moment when she would have to climb into the back seat of the sedan that pulled up at the end of the evening to take her home. Then Dawn had delivered her new baby girl in early March, and Angel understandably heard from her far less often. Patrice had found a new guy and now spent much of her time with him.

Yes, the drapes were opened up early each morning and she now planned the daily menus with Olivia, who was always accommodating. When Angel learned Olivia was a master of African- and Asian-inspired cuisines, she encouraged her to add them to the menus. So, lots of okra, plantain, fish, rice, and noodles popped up on their dinner plates, to Everett's delight. Angel had even spruced up the primary-bedroom decor with the help of an interior decorator, adding cheerful bed linens, drapes, and wall hangings. Anything to try and counter the doom and gloom surrounding her.

Yet she still had way too much idle time. She was a woman who was used to twelve-hour workdays. When she mentioned her boredom to Everett, he suggested she hire a coach for tennis lessons to be ready to play on the courts later in the spring or daily laps in the indoor pool. She toyed with these ideas, but they really weren't her thing. She needed to be creative or to work with her hands. Which was why she found cooking so appealing. Something like tennis would never satisfy her. She thought of going back to her soups and salads cookbook but without regular access to a kitchen of her own, that would be pointless. Olivia was kind enough to allow her to slip into the kitchen now and then for an hour or two to whip up a dish. But that was not nearly enough for testing recipes. In this house, the kitchen was Olivia's domain; Angel didn't want to intrude too much.

It wasn't exactly a hobby, but strolling the grounds at River-wild soon became her go-to activity whenever the loneliness really got to her. She loved experiencing the gardens through-out the seasons, letting her imagination run freely. When winter hit, the trees went bare and the river came into stark view with the sunlight glistening on the surface. Early spring now brought new life everywhere she looked. Her walks grew more frequent, soon becoming a daily ritual, especially when Everett was out of town. She would slip into a pair of ankle boots or tennis shoes with a light jacket and dash out to catch the fresh breezes.

Once or twice a week on her walks she ran into Ethan and his crew putting around in the flower and herb gardens. He had been employed there since July the year previous, arriving not long before Angel had. He was medium height, very fit, and handsome in a rugged sort of way. She figured he was somewhere in his late thirties, early forties. At first, they only nodded when they came across each other. Soon the nods became smiles and warm greetings.

When he caught her picking herbs from the garden one after-noon while Everett was away, he dropped his wheelbarrow and offered to help.

"Oh no. I enjoy doing it myself," she said, inhaling the pungent menthol scent of green mint leaves.

"Olivia sometimes comes out here, too," Ethan said. "She likes to use the herbs in her cooking."

"So she told me. I was going to take these to her. Or maybe I'll do something with them myself. You and your crew do an amazing job out here, Ethan. I've been meaning to tell you that. Everything is kept so well year-round."

"Thank you, ma'am," he said, smiling with appreciation. "Can't believe I get paid to be out here doing something I love. I consider myself lucky."

Her mind quickly turned to her days in the kitchen at Georgia's. "Yes, you are. I miss that."

"Yes, I see you out here enjoying the gardens, too."

"I meant cooking. I was once a chef, believe it or not. Loved it, although I haven't done much lately."

He blinked with astonishment. "You? A chef?"

She chuckled at his reaction and nodded. "I worked for several years in a restaurant in DC."

"You don't look nothing like a cook."

She laughed. "I'm not sure how to take that."

"It's a compliment. You look like the lady of the estate. I never would have imagined much else."

"Thank you. I gave up cooking when I got married."

"Ah. I don't think I could ever give up gardening. Even if I didn't need the money, I would still be out digging around in the dirt, planting new stuff, watching everything grow."

She smiled. "I completely understand. I do get into the kitchen once in a while."

"Oh? Here at Riverwild?"

"Mm-hmm."

"My wife, Tina, she loves to bake."

"What's your wife's favorite dessert to make?"

"I don't know her favorite to make but I know what my favorite is to eat," he said, laughing. "Her pies. The kids would probably say cookies."

Angel laughed, and for a moment, she envied Ethan and his simple, loving family life. "How many children do you have?"

"Three," he said with pride. "Two sons, a daughter. Seven, five, and two."

"How nice! I'll bring you a couple of pie and cookie recipes next time I'm out here. That is, if you think your wife would like that."

"She would love that, ma'am."

"What kind of pie would you like for yourself?"

"Apple," he said happily. "Or peach."

"I'll bring them later this week. Chocolate chip cookies seem to be the biggest hit with kids at their ages."

He nodded enthusiastically. "Can't thank you enough, ma'am. If there's anything special you ever want planted around the garden or anywhere out here, just let me know. Mostly I take directions from the other Mrs. Bruce but . . ."

Angel stiffened; the light mood suddenly shifted. "You mean Miss Bruce."

Ethan hesitated for a few seconds. She could tell that he was trying to figure out what had just happened. Then it seemed to hit him. He nodded. "Yes, Mrs. Bruce. If you want something special done, don't hesitate to ask. I'm all ears."

"Thank you, Ethan. I'll keep that in mind."

She turned toward the house and a sadness welled up inside her, unlike on other days, when these walks left her feeling momentarily invigorated. Talking to Ethan about his joyful life, filled with the love of his family, had gotten to her. For all the wealth and status she had acquired since marrying Everett, what was lacking was true, unbridled happiness in the simple things.

* * *

As Angel approached the stairs to the rear door, she noticed Everett watching her from the primary bedroom window above. She smiled, blew him a kiss, pleasantly surprised to see him home a day early from his business trip. She picked up her pace and skipped up the stairs. Indoors, she handed her jacket and the freshly picked mint to Jackson, instructing him to make sure Olivia got the herbs. Then she took the elevator up.

Her wide smile faded the second she caught her husband's dour expression as he turned away from the window. He was still in a suit and tie, his briefcase at his feet. From his dressing room nearby, she could hear drawers opening and shutting as his valet unpacked and put away his belongings.

"James," Everett called, raising his voice to be heard in the distance.

The valet entered the bedroom. "Yes, sir?"

"Excuse us, please. Come back in about thirty minutes."

James, dressed in slacks and a crisp collared shirt, walked briskly across the room and out the door.

"Is everything all right?" she asked from just inside the doorway after James passed by.

She could feel Everett's eyes boring into her. It felt like he was inspecting her, examining her, from her green woolen pullover to the faded jeans. It made her uncomfortable. She had no idea what to think. Or what he was thinking. Clearly something was troubling him. She edged closer. "Everett?"

"What was that all about?" His voice was low, terse.

She shook her head slowly, feeling confused. "What was *what* all about?"

He gestured toward the window. "Where were you coming from just now?"

"From out . . . I went for a walk around here like I always do."

"What do you and Ethan have so much to gab about?"

"I . . . you mean the gardener? We . . ." She paused, momentarily speechless at the sneer that suddenly spread across his face.

"You know of any other Ethans around here?"

Whoa. What was with the harsh tone? "What has gotten into you? We were chatting about dessert recipes. He was telling me about his wife and three kids."

He shoved his fists into the pockets of his slacks, twisted his bottom lip. "You're being too damn friendly with the help."

"Excuse me?"

"Ethan is the help. Not your friend."

She scoffed as a wave of frustration flared up within her. "Maybe because I once *was* the help, I can easily relate."

"Or maybe you don't need to flirt so damn much."

"What the hell is wrong with you, Ev?"

He grimaced, gritted his teeth.

"Look," she added, "I don't know what this is about but I damn sure know I have not done anything wrong."

"You're too much like her."

She flinched, not sure where this was going. She had heard him say that before, never in a good way.

"I thought I could trust that you would be different," he continued. "I should have known better. You were probably still with your ex-boyfriend when we met, even though you said you weren't. I've always suspected that."

She gulped. She hadn't thought about Gene or her little lie in months.

"Well? Were you?"

"I . . . I mean, we were close to breaking up."

He exhaled loudly. "So you lied. Figures."

"I broke up with him completely right after we met. Before you and I became a couple."

He ignored her. "Women. Can any of you be trusted?"

"I'm not sure what you're implying but . . ."

"Chloe slept around with everyone, including the gardener. It never stopped."

She hadn't seen that coming. "That's not fair. I don't know about Chloe, but I've never cheated on you. Never will. And Ethan said he just started working here back in July. She couldn't have been with him."

"Not Ethan. The one before him."

She paused. She wanted Everett to continue but was almost afraid of what he might say. "What . . . what happened with the previous gardener?"

His brows creased as he thought. But instead of replying, he bent down, snatched up his briefcase, and brushed past her toward the door. She reached out, touched his arm. "Did she have an affair with him?"

He shook her hand off, refused to look into her face. "What do you think?"

"I'm not like Chloe, Everett."

He gave her a doubtful look and exited the room. She thought of chasing after him, of trying to right this stupid misunderstanding. Then decided against it. She knew now that whenever he got like this, it was impossible to reach him. The hold that Chloe still had over him was unbelievable. The woman was long dead and buried, yet she might as well be running around the halls of Riverwild the way Everett behaved. Ida, too. Angel could feel her presence hovering over them all, day after day, night after night. Just as Ida had said, her aura lingered in every room. It was uncanny. And she was sick and tired of it.

She desperately needed to get to the bottom of all this strangeness. But how? She was never going to get anything out of the two of them. She would have to find another way. She glanced at her watch. Three o'clock. This was when Janetta, the maid who cleaned the upstairs bedrooms, dusted and vacuumed Chloe's room every other day, like clockwork. Ida's orders.

Angel clenched her fists with determination and exited the room. She took the elevator down to the lower level and briskly walked down the long hallway, stopping at the door to Chloe's bedroom.

* * *

It was partially open, a sign that Janetta was inside. Sometimes she could hear Ida's voice coming from the room, ordering Janetta around as she went about her chores. Angel stepped closer to listen. The only sound was soft footsteps walking back and forth across the wood floor.

She pushed on the door. Janetta gasped when she saw her. Angel assumed she was not used to seeing the face of anyone besides Ida enter this precious sanctuary.

"Mrs. Bruce," Janetta said, barely above a whisper. "What can I do for you?" She lowered the dust cloth from the small desk she had been cleaning.

It was uncanny how everyone in the house whispered and tiptoed around in fear of Ida's wrath. "Hello, Janetta. You can take a break."

"Seriously? But I'm not done in here yet."

"Come back and finish up in about half an hour."

Janetta took a reluctant step toward the doorway. "If you say so."

"And, Janetta, keep this between us." Angel didn't want Janetta running off to tell Ida before she had time to look around.

"Yes, Mrs. Bruce."

Angel stood in the middle of the floor at the foot of a huge four-poster wooden bed and slowly turned about. The expansive room was decorated with off-white furniture and plush rugs and bedding in shades of lilac and cream. What most surprisingly caught Angel's attention were the lilac window treatments. They were all wide open, allowing bright rays of sunlight to warm the space. How odd, Angel thought. How strange. Every other room in the house had been as dark as a tomb before she'd made changes, whereas this space was light, open, airy.

Not only that but Chloe's personal belongings were all still in place, sitting atop her dresser, desk, and nightstands, as if she were expected to return at any moment. On the vanity, her hairbrush and comb sat neatly next to a bejeweled hand mirror surrounded by makeup and perfume bottles. Two jewelry boxes stuffed to the brim with gold and diamond adornments rested on top of her dresser. Next to that was a silver-framed portrait of a smiling Everett.

Finally, Angel looked up and scanned an almost life-size gold-framed painting on the wall opposite the bed. In it, Chloe stood on the landing at the top of the grand staircase at River-wild Estate. Her tall, slender figure was dressed in an exquisite low-cut purple ball gown. Her auburn hair was piled on top of her head, adorned with a diamond and pearl tiara. Talk about over-the-top. Angel thought it all a bit too much.

"She looks regal, doesn't she?"

A chill crawled up Angel's spine. The voice nearly knocked her off her feet. She pivoted to see her sister-in-law standing in the doorway, arms folded lightly across her waist, eyes gazing adoringly at the painting. Surprisingly, Ida seemed calm. How long had she been standing there? Angel wondered.

"Yes," Angel said. "She looks lovely. When was that painted?"

"The photograph was taken in the last year of their marriage, during the annual dinner and ball they held here every spring. The tiara was an anniversary gift from Everett. I had someone create the painting from the photograph after she died."

Angel nodded. "Very nice."

"She was perfect in every way."

Angel cleared her throat. She wouldn't go that far. "Is it always so bright in here? It's a big difference from how the rest of the house was kept."

Ida smiled thinly. "Everything in here has been left just as it was when Chloe was alive. She always wanted the drapes opened first thing in the morning."

"Really?"

"She loved letting the light in."

"Oh." Just like her, Angel thought. As Everett might have said. "I see."

"It was my decision to keep the drapes closed in the rest of the house after she passed away."

"I understand, although I'm not sure I agree with having them like that for so long. Especially for Everett. This place seems to trigger bad memories for him. He has terrible nightmares. Keeping it dark all the time can't have helped."

Ida shifted stiffly from one foot to the other. "Perhaps."

"I understand that you and Chloe were very close but . . ."

"Yes, we were," Ida said, glancing lovingly toward the portrait as she spoke.

"She's been dead for nearly two years now and . . ." Angel paused as Ida suddenly threw a far less loving gaze filled with daggers toward her.

"Will that be all?" Ida asked, plainly, simply, coldly.

Angel backed silently out of the room. If she had thought the fleeting amiable chat between the two of them might lead to a thaw in their relationship, she was dead wrong.

17

"That wife of yours is dangerous, Everett. I'm worried."

"What are you talking about? She's fine."

"I'm not so sure about that. Caught her snooping in Chloe's room.

"When was this?"

"Yesterday."

Silence. Loud sigh. "I thought you kept that locked up, Ida."

"She snuck in while Janetta was cleaning. I'm telling you, Everett, she's gotten much too bold for her own good. How much does she know? What have you told her about that night?"

"Nothing. Not a single thing. Anyway, I thought you said you were going to clean the room out, Ida."

"I will. When I'm ready." Deep sigh. "I need to do it myself and haven't had the heart to go through her things just yet."

"Then at least get rid of her personal papers. Who knows what Chloe kept."

"You're right. This wasn't a big problem until you brought *her* here."

"Never mind that. If you can't take care of the room soon, I'll have someone else do it."

"No. I'll get it done this afternoon."

"See that you do. I have to get going now. I'm already late for work."

Angel backed away from the doorway to Everett's office and slid around the corner as quickly and quietly as she could. She lingered inside the library until she heard her husband, and finally Ida, walk by. Only then did she allow herself to exhale.

What had she just overheard? And what did it all mean?

That wife of yours is dangerous.

What have you told her about that night?

Get rid of her personal papers.

Told her about *what?* Angel wondered. And about which night?

She tossed the words over and over in her mind. Nothing she could think of made sense but she didn't have much time to try and figure it out. She needed to get inside Chloe's room before Ida cleared it out. Janetta was not due to clean again until tomorrow and by then it might be too late. She had to get in there today. Now.

She flew down the hallway after Ida to see where she was headed. She was forced to stop dead in her tracks and retreat quickly when she saw Ida coming straight toward her as she re-entered the mansion from a side door. Fortunately, Ida was busy going through a ring of at least a dozen keys in her hand and hadn't noticed her. Angel had seen that ring hanging from a hook on the wall near the desk in the cottage. One of them was likely the key to Chloe's room and Ida was probably headed there. Angel had visons of sneaking up behind Ida, overpowering her, and snatching the key ring as she helplessly watched Ida slip farther and farther down the hallway. How would she ever get her hands on those keys?

Then Jackson appeared suddenly from around another corner. "Ida," he said. "I've been looking all over for you. You have a visitor. Mrs.—"

Ida waved Jackson off, passing him without stopping. "Tell whoever it is to wait," she said gruffly. "Or get rid of them. I need to check on something."

"But it's Mrs. Clarke, Chloe's mom. She says she isn't going anywhere until she speaks to you."

Ida stopped, turned to face Jackson. "What? She hasn't been here in months. I thought she was done bothering us. Dammit. That woman is going to drive me insane. What the hell does she want after all this time?"

Jackson shrugged.

"Here," Ida said, shoving the keys toward him. "Take these. Make sure Chloe's room is locked. I got distracted yesterday when I found that foolish woman in there and may have forgotten to lock it after Janetta was done cleaning."

"You mean Angel, ma'am?"

"Of course. Who else?"

They parted and headed in opposite directions, Ida toward the main entrance, Jackson up the stairs to the guest room level. Angel did not at all appreciate the way Ida had spoken about her to Jackson. It was disrespectful, uncalled for. But she wasn't surprised and didn't have time to stress over that now. Should she follow Jackson and try to get the keys? Or Ida, to learn what Chloe's mom was there about? She knew from reading the papers about the night Chloe died that her parents did not believe their daughter had taken her own life.

Angel decided to take her chances with Jackson and quickly took off after him. She ran up to the top landing, paused breathlessly, and peered around the corner, watching him as he continued down the hallway. He stopped in front of Chloe's room and tried the doorknob; it didn't budge. He double-checked. It was clearly already locked. He turned around to head back. That's when Angel made her move.

"Jackson," she said, stepping out in front of him.

He leaped back, nearly tripping over his own feet. She had obviously startled him, but he recovered quickly. "Mrs. Bruce. What can I do for you?"

Her eyes roamed down to his hands. "Do you have the key to Chloe's room there?"

"Um, yes. I was just . . ."

"Oh, good. I'll take it. I need to check for something."

"Ma'am, I'm not sure that Miss Bruce . . ."

"Who?"

He paused, swallowed hard.

She took a step forward and held out her palm, hoping to high heaven that it wouldn't start trembling. That she looked firm, commanding. She must have because Jackson immediately gave her the ring of keys, holding up the one to Chloe's room.

"Thank you," she said. "I'll make sure to lock up when I'm done."

He nodded, scurried off. She released a gust of air, feeling good about having finally perfected the look that said "I'm *Mrs.* Bruce. I'm in charge around here."

But she didn't have a lot of time to dwell on her burgeoning authoritativeness. Jackson no doubt would tell Ida what had just happened as soon as the guest departed. She had to move quickly. She inserted the key, swung the door open. Once inside, she closed the door and glanced around, not sure where to start. She had no idea what she was even looking for. No idea what she might find. She tossed the key ring on top of the dresser and started pulling drawers open. One by one, trying to be as quiet as possible. Then she moved to the nightstands and desk. She saw clothing, makeup, jewelry. In the desk she found stationery, pens, and a couple of loose photographs of Chloe with her parents and friends. Nothing unexpected.

She was about to enter the walk-in closet when she heard footsteps approaching outside the doorway. Her spine went cold. She froze, held her breath. Ida? Here already? She tiptoed to the door, cracked it open slowly, peered down the hallway. It was only Janetta entering one of the other guest bedrooms. Thank goodness.

She opened the double doors to the closet to find a dressing area larger than her condo. Designer labels were everywhere, from the floor-to-ceiling shoe racks to the shelves stuffed with handbags. Manolo Blahnik, Jimmy Choo, Christian Louboutin, and on and on. An entire wall was devoted to Hermès bags in every color you could imagine. Her eyes finally settled on the built-in drawers extending along the center of the room. She opened them all, one after the other. More designer scarves and lingerie but nothing of note. She was beginning to think that maybe there was nothing to be found.

She exited the dressing room area and grabbed the keys. She was about to head to the door when she looked up and caught the life-size portrait of Chloe staring down from the wall, a mesmerizing vision in purple and a tiara. It seemed a little foolish to hope the painting could offer some kind of clue about where to search, but Angel was getting desperate for *something*. She hooked onto Chloe's light eyes and followed them downward toward the desk. Something suddenly nagged at her, urged her to check it once more. It was an elegant white piece with intricate golden trim. Despite its size it had only three drawers. Instinct told her that some of the interior space was unaccounted for. She noted that the lower right-hand portion of the desk was a decorative panel with gold inlay. She dropped the keys and leaned in closely, pulled at each of the four corners. The panel didn't budge. She pressed on one of the corners. A door flew open.

She gasped. Her heart raced with anticipation. She glanced

nervously toward the doorway to make sure she was still alone. Then she knelt down, looked inside. There were two shelves. On the top shelf lay a small pile of papers. The lower shelf held an intricately decorated gold letter box. She pulled the box out, sat it on top of the desk and tugged at the lid. It was locked. "Shoot," she whispered under her breath. That's when she remembered the keys. She grabbed them and tried a little gold key that matched the color of the box. The top popped up.

Inside was a stack of letters neatly tied together with a purple ribbon. She flipped through and saw that the handwriting on the front of all of them read: *My Darling Chloe.* Angel immediately noted that it did not appear to be Everett's writing; Chloe had had her share of lovers. At least two that Angel was aware of. She hesitated. Opening the private correspondence would be prying, sticking her nose where it didn't belong. But she couldn't stop herself. They might help her understand some of the strangeness going on around here. What everyone was so guarded and secretive about. Why Chloe held so much sway, even from her grave. Angel told herself she would glance at only one or two of the letters to see who they were from.

She carefully pulled one out from the middle of the pile and quickly scanned it. She couldn't help but note the flowery prose pouring forth from the page; the *I love you*s, the *I can't live without you*s. She shook her head. So troubling that this had been written to Everett's then-wife. The same for the panting recollections of sexy, passion-filled nights spent together. Sad, really.

But the signature at the bottom of the page that stabbed Angel's eyes was another story.

Yours forever, Ida.

Angel's breath caught in her throat. She stared off into space, tried to make sense of what she'd just read. Then suddenly, it *did* make sense. Absolute, complete, total sense. This explained so much. Ida had been madly in love with Chloe. And the two of them had been having an affair. Angel pulled out a couple more envelopes from the top of the pile. Both were love letters from Ida to Chloe, filled with more of the same. The dates indicated that the affair had lasted for at least a year.

This was beyond surreal. It was horrible. Did Everett have any idea? Seemed unlikely since he and his sister were so close. And if so, he had never mentioned a word to her. But that didn't mean he was unaware. He hid so much.

She shut the box abruptly, pulled out the documents on the top shelf and quickly flipped through them, the clock ticking loudly in her head. Notes, pamphlets, schedules. One item caught her attention. A one-way first-class airline ticket in Chloe's name to Cabo San Lucas International Airport, dated for the week following her death. So, Chloe had been planning a trip to Mexico? And she was flying commercial rather than using their private jet? No one had ever mentioned this. Not Everett, not Ida. Were they aware?

She reopened the letter box, removed the one at the top. It quickly became obvious that Ida did know Chloe had been planning an extended trip to Mexico without either Everett or herself. The first lines read:

I don't understand why you refuse to take me with you to Mexico. We've been together for so long, and I have no interest in staying here indefinitely without you.

Angel sank into the desk chair. She needed a moment to steady her racing thoughts. Had Everett been aware of Chloe's plans? Had Chloe finally agreed to Ida's wishes? Or denied them? Angel needed time to absorb all this. But not now. She had to shut all this down, get out of there, and return the keys to Jackson without detection. Ida had walked in on her in this room once; that could not happen again.

She stood and stuffed two of the letters and the airline ticket into the back pockets of her jeans. Then she carefully but rapidly replaced everything else—the remaining letters, the box, the stack of papers—just as she'd found them. She closed and locked the secret-panel door and headed out in search of Jackson.

He was walking briskly up the stairs when she caught up to him. Hopefully he had not yet spoken to Ida. She approached him, held out the key ring.

"I'm done now, Jackson. Thank you."

"Of course. Did you find what you needed, ma'am?"

"I certainly did. Have you seen Ida around?"

"I believe she's still downstairs with a guest."

Angel nodded. So Chloe's mom was still there, and Jackson likely had not talked to her. "Thank you, Jackson."

"No trouble at all."

"And, Jackson." Angel smiled. "Let's keep this with the keys between us. Ida does not need to know."

Jackson hesitated then bowed his head slightly, "Of course, Mrs. Bruce."

* * *

"I'm so sorry I can't be of more help, Paulette," Ida was saying. Angel was lurking around the corner, near the door to the parlor where Chloe's mom and Ida were meeting. With her back pressed tightly against the wall, she was close enough to hear but far enough to remain out of sight.

"Like I said," Ida continued, her voice coming clearly, thanks to the high ceilings. "We haven't heard from Damon since he left last year. We've had a couple of other gardeners since then."

"You haven't answered my question, Ida. Had you heard that he and my daughter were having an affair? Because I just recently learned about it. Of course, I'm her mother. She would never have told me about something like this."

Silence. Then, "No, absolutely not. And I seriously doubt that it's true. Where in the world did you hear that?"

"My new cleaning woman, Antonia. She insists they were seeing each other. There have been rumors ever since her death that Chloe was involved with someone else. But you know, I always dismissed them. I thought it was absurd. I knew she and Everett were having problems, but I never believed my daughter would have an affair. Then Antonia showed me a photo of the two of them together that she had on her cell phone. They were at a bar in DC."

"I . . . I find that hard to believe."

Angel wondered if this affair with the gardener was news to Ida, or if like Everett, she had known about it all along, too. Angel had seen no mention of Damon in the letters, but that didn't mean Ida was unaware of him.

"Antonia also said the reason Damon left was because Everett fired him when he found out," Paulette said.

"Paulette, please. Stop this. I highly doubt that. Everett fired him because he was incompetent. Anyway, what are you implying?"

"Could Damon have had something to do with my daughter's death? Maybe he was angry and snuck back in here that night to confront her. They argued and . . ."

"So, you're thinking Damon shot Chloe?"

"I think it's possible. He was fired a few weeks before her death."

"Um, no, Paulette. Everett and I both ran immediately to her bedroom when we heard the gunshot. She was alone. The gun was on the floor near her hand."

"He could have staged it and run off before you got there."

"Look, I know it's hard for you to accept, but Chloe had been despondent for some time and . . ."

"Chloe despondent? No way. That's simply not true. The last time she visited us, two days before she died, she was in great spirits. She was smiling and all excited about getting away."

"So you've said."

"Yes. Well, who commits suicide just before a big trip? I think Damon killed her. He became upset because he was fired or maybe because she was leaving him. I don't know, but if they were having an affair around the time of her death, I do know one thing. He needs to be investigated by the police. Don't you agree?"

"Paulette, I'm going to have to ask you to leave. You're making wild, baseless assumptions."

"Fine then. I won't bother you any longer. I'll just take this new information to the police myself."

"Do as you see fit."

Angel heard footsteps and peeked around the corner to see Ida and Paulette emerge from the room. Paulette looked like an older version of Chloe, a little shorter and heavier, with a head full of auburn hair cut into a sleek bob. She appeared to be dressed in upscale designers from head to toe—suit, bag, heels. Like mother, like daughter, Angel thought.

Ida stood stiffly inside the doorway of the parlor and watched as Paulette followed Jackson to the front door. Angel hoped Ida would leave the area so she could catch up to Paulette. She would love a chance to speak to Chloe's mom and maybe learn a little more about the woman who seemed to have cast a spell over them all. But the opportunity was slipping away quickly as Ida watched Paulette's every footstep, heels clacking down the hallway. Well after Jackson had shut the doors, Ida stood in her spot, appearing deep in thought.

Finally, Ida made her way toward a side exit leading down to her cottage. Angel rounded the corner and dashed to the front doors. She pulled them wide open only to catch the back of a late-model dark-gray Mercedes sedan heading down the driveway. Dammit, Angel thought, stomping her foot. But she was not about to give up easily on an opportunity to talk to someone outside of this household who knew Chloe well, given all she had just learned.

Chloe had been having an affair shortly before her death with the gardener, and Paulette knew about it, had even learned that the man's name was Damon. Chloe had been planning a lengthy trip, seemingly without her husband or any of her lovers—Ida, Damon, or Reggie. And the biggest, most shocking revelation of all— Chloe and Ida had been having a long-term affair. Did Paulette know anything more about the trip or about the other affairs?

Angel entered Everett's office and pulled his business card book out from where she knew he kept it, the top right-hand drawer of his desk. She flipped through until she came to a card from Chloe's dad's neurosurgery practice. On the back someone had scribbled the Clarke's personal address. Angel was familiar with the upscale Northwest DC neighborhood of stately older homes built during the twentieth century.

She wanted to keep her little excursion secret for now, so she ordered the BMW, one of the smaller cars from the fleet parked in the garage, to be brought out front. Everett had mentioned that this was the car Chloe preferred when she wanted to drive somewhere alone.

She carefully changed out of her jeans and into a designer dress that still had the tags on it, one that Everett had purchased for her shortly after the wedding. She had caught a glimpse of something similar—same deep purple color, same sleek shape—in Chloe's closet. The dress, like others, had sat unworn for months because it wasn't Angel's style. They were far too expensive to wear when hanging out with her friends from DC. She mainly wore them when dining out with Everett or attending gatherings with his friends and business acquaintances. That happened far less often of late. For some reason, the dress felt entirely appropriate for a visit with Chloe's mom. She reached for her violet Kelly bag and five minutes later strolled across the courtyard and slipped behind the wheel of a vehicle for the first time in months.

18

Forty minutes later, Angel cruised down a busy, tree-lined Six-teenth Street in DC, breezing by twentieth-century colonials, ramblers, and split-levels. She turned onto a side street and drove along slowly until she reached a large brick Tudor-style house where the same gray Mercedes Paulette had driven off in earlier sat in the driveway. She pulled to the curb, made her way up the walkway, and rang the bell. At the sound of footsteps approach-ing, her stomach did a little somersault. She had no idea how Chloe's mom would react to meeting her former son-in-law's new wife. Chloe's replacement.

Paulette peered through a clear section of the stained-glass side panel. "Yes?" came the voice through the video doorbell. "Can I help you?"

"Hello." Angel cleared her now dry-as-sandpaper throat. "I'm Angel, Everett's wife." She smiled, shifted from one heel to the other. "I saw you as you were leaving the house earlier today but couldn't catch up to you. I'd love a chance to talk, Mrs. Clarke. If you have time."

Paulette observed her silently for a moment. Then Angel heard the locks clicking, and the door cracked ajar. The expression on Paulette's face seemed mixed—part surprise, part curiosity.

"I know this isn't the best circumstance for us to meet," Angel said, smiling broadly. "But I couldn't help but overhear some of your conversation with Ida."

"You heard us?" Paulette said, eyeing Angel up and down. "Why didn't you introduce yourself then?"

Angel's smile thinned. "It's complicated."

"Hmm. I'll bet. *Everything* at that house has always been so complicated. Well, come on in. Maybe you can fill in some blanks about what's been going on over there for me."

Paulette led her through a wide hallway past rooms filled with Persian carpets and silver-framed artwork. They entered a great room with a towering wood-beamed ceiling and two seating areas. Angel followed Paulette to the smaller area next to a roaring fireplace and sat in one of the stuffed armchairs. Her heels sank deeply into an expensive-looking carpet.

"Can I get you something to drink?" Paulette asked before sitting.

Angel shook her head. "Thank you, I'm fine." She was anxious to get this going. To learn more about the woman who had so much influence on her life, even from her grave.

Paulette sat directly across from Angel, crossed her legs at the ankles. Up close, Angel noticed that she had soft features and a smooth, creamy complexion. Very few wrinkles. She wore more makeup than Chloe had in her photos, but that might be expected given that Paulette was an older woman.

"So. What brings you here?"

"First, I'm so sorry about what happened with your daughter."

Paulette nodded. "Thank you. You know, you remind me of her in a way."

Angel blinked. She was not expecting to hear that. Based on the painting at the house, she could not see it. Her hair was shorter, darker, and wavier, her complexion a few shades browner.

"I don't mean physically," Paulette added, seeming to note Angel's skepticism. "There's something about your aura, the way you carry yourself. You have a sweet but strong presence, which is how I always thought of Chloe. Everett obviously has a type."

"Oh. Well, thank you."

"How have things been going for you at Riverwild?"

"Let's just say, I'm adjusting. Your daughter's presence is still very much felt in the house."

"I've sensed that myself. It's been several months since I was there, but I could see today that not much has changed. Except they finally opened those damn drapes."

"That was my doing."

"Good for you. I should think as his new wife you would want to put your stamp on things."

"It hasn't been easy."

Paulette lifted her brows. "Because of Everett?"

"Mmm. Not really."

"Oh, I see. Yes, Ida can be very, let's say, stubborn. Inflexible. The only one she ever really listened to was Chloe. Not even her brother had much sway. But I'm sure you'll figure things out. After all, you are his wife."

"I'm trying. Mrs. Clarke, can I get right to the point of why I came here today?"

Paulette cocked her head to the side. "Please do."

"Based on what I overheard earlier, you seem fairly sure that Chloe did not, um . . ."

"Commit suicide?"

"Yes."

Paulette squared her shoulders. "I'm positive. She would never, ever have done such a thing."

"What makes you so certain?"

"I know my daughter. She hated guns. Absolutely hated them. I can't see her even touching one."

"Everett says she was depressed."

"Hmph. I don't know why the hell he would say that. Now, she and Everett had not been happy with each other for a while. Oh, they put on a good show for the world, but we talked, my daughter and I. She was becoming more and more disillusioned with their marriage, but she was not depressed."

"Why do you think they were so unhappy?"

"They were complete opposites. He's more reserved, all business."

Angel nodded in agreement.

"Chloe on the other hand was an extrovert. Very passionate. A people person. She was an only child, you know, and probably far too indulged. Francis, her dad, was a neurosurgeon. He worked hours on end and tried to make up for his frequent absences by showering us both with gifts—clothes, jewelry, trips. Anything and everything we ever wanted. He could never say no to his daughter."

"I see."

Paulette looked into Angel's eyes. "What do you think of Riverwild, Angel?"

"Amazing place. Magical."

Paulette scoffed. "Well, it should be. He paid nearly fifty million bucks for it, as I'm sure you know. At Chloe's insistence. Ridiculous, if you ask me. Even if he is a billionaire."

Angel smiled.

"But that was Chloe. She could never, ever have enough. Always wanting more. But she was charming, funny, outgoing. Men adored her. Women wanted to be like her. And she usually got what she wanted."

Angel thought back to the portrait and how imposing Chloe

looked in it. "There's a huge, almost life-size painting of her in one of the bedrooms. She looks stunning."

"Yes, I know the one you're referring to. That was one of my favorite images of her. It hung downstairs in one of the parlors for a while shortly after she died. Than Ida moved it upstairs and I haven't seen it since." Paulette's eyes filled with tears.

Angel reached into her bag and pulled out a couple of tissues. "Sorry," she said, handing them to Paulette. "If this is too much to talk about . . ."

"Not at all. There's nothing I enjoy talking about more than my Chloe." Paulette sniffed, dabbed at her eyes. "Before they married, she was a celebrity photographer, you know, met a lot of people. She seemed to fall in love with a new man every six months. Rich, poor. She didn't discriminate in that way. I used to say she was in love with love. Her father blamed himself for her spoiled, somewhat reckless ways. I always called her my wild child."

Angel smiled at Paulette's use of the words as a term of endearment.

"By the time she met Everett, she was in her mid-thirties, and when he proposed and got her to settle down, we were beyond thrilled. Francis and I thanked him for finally taking our daughter off the streets. He obviously cared deeply about her, and we knew he could take care of her, spoil her in the way she desired."

Paulette paused and her mood seemed to grow more pensive. "The marriage was also kind of an arrangement. She never said that, but it worked out that way. He brought the money, and a lot of it. But it was new money. She brought the right long-established local connections; her dad was very well-known and respected in Washington and beyond, especially in Black circles. The marriage seemed like a match made in heaven and it worked beautifully for a while. They were a much sought-after couple, invited everywhere. They entertained at Riverwild all the time. Their annual spring ball was legendary. The painting you speak of was based on a photo taken during the last ball before her death."

Paulette glanced downward and her expression turned sad. "By that time, the marriage had been in serious trouble for months, years even. Although they both hid it well in public."

"What do you think happened?"

"Their differences started to come out more. Chloe came to realize that Everett was a lot like her dad in that he worked non-stop and was never going to change. He would buy her these lavish, insanely expensive gifts to try and make up for being away so much. Cars, jewelry. Far bigger and grander than anything her father could ever afford. It was probably exciting for her at first, but she eventually became tired of it."

Angel nodded. "Everett said he wanted to have children. She didn't."

"That, too. He wanted to start a family, which is understandable. She was approaching forty, didn't have a lot of time. I agreed with him on that. I wanted grandbabies. But Chloe was adamant she would not be rushed, always pointing out all the new medical advances that she could use when she was ready. I think she was scared to death of children forcing her to slow down and live a different lifestyle. Eventually they began to spend just about all their time apart. He was always on business trips and she started to travel for her charities."

And at some point during all the discord, Angel thought, Chloe started having the affairs. Reggie. Damon. Ida. And who knew how many others. Chloe's mom could well be in the dark about all of them except Damon, so Angel would not mention the others or the pregnancy and miscarriage. Paulette was likely unaware of just how wild her daughter really was, and Angel certainly wasn't going to be the one to inform her. That would serve no purpose at all, only further worry a mother already heart-broken over the loss of her only child.

"Disagreeing on having children can be a strain on any marriage," Angel said.

Paulette nodded. "Oh, it can be a deal-breaker. I don't know how much you heard of my conversation with Ida but the last time we saw Chloe, she was so excited about an upcoming trip to Cabo San Lucas. She wanted to get away and loved that area."

Angel nodded. "I heard a little about that." Not entirely a lie. She'd actually *read* about it in Ida's secret love letters to Chloe.

"She even put a down payment on a house near the beach the week before she died."

Angel's eyes widened. This she did not know. "Really? I had no idea."

"She paid almost five million for it and couldn't wait to get down there to start fixing it up. I was planning to spend some time there to help her. That's one of many reasons I don't believe for a second that she committed suicide. No one buys property a week before they take their own life."

Angel nodded. "I had no idea. Does Everett know about this?"

"No, they don't know anything about it because she put the property in my name. Chloe wanted it that way so that if the marriage didn't work out, Everett would not be able to get his hands on it. That's why I kept quiet about it all this time. As you probably heard, I just found out about Chloe's relationship with one of the gardeners. What was his name again?"

"Damon."

"Yes, him. This seventy-year-old mind isn't what it used to be when it comes to names. Anyway, what if he was upset that she was leaving and wanted to stop her, so he killed her? Or maybe it was an accident. I don't know but the police need to be made aware of this. And letting them know about the property she bought just before dying will help prove that she would not have committed suicide."

"Oh, wow." Angel decided not to tell Paulette that she was also starting to believe that Chloe had met her death at the hands of a jealous, possessive lover. But not Damon. Somehow, Angel suspected the relationship between them was a casual, short-term fling with little emotional attachment. No, she suspected her sister-in-law. Ida had been madly in love with Chloe, knew she was leaving for Mexico, and had desperately begged not to be left behind. The proof was right there in the letters and airline ticket now tucked away in a drawer in her bedroom closet. But before Angel mentioned her thoughts to anyone, she had to talk to her husband. And that was not going to be easy.

"What happened with the property?" Angel asked. She wanted all the details before talking to Everett.

Paulette sighed with regret. "I struggled to keep up with the payments and had to put it on the market. It sold last month. I really did not want to do that. It was one of the few things I had left from her, but I had no choice."

Angel nodded. "I understand."

"It's frustrating that Everett has accepted suicide so willingly and won't pursue this any further. Chloe's dad didn't believe it either. He had retired by then, spent all of his time chasing down leads before he died. I think that's what killed him."

"I'm really sorry to hear that."

Paulette leaned in closer. "With this new information about my daughter's affair with the gardener and the property she purchased in Mexico, I'm seriously considering going to the police and telling them everything I know. What do you think?"

Angel racked her brain. Personally, she thought the whole thing with Damon was far-fetched and wouldn't go very far with the police. Her idea about what had happened was much more likely to be taken seriously.

"I'm going to bring this up with Everett tonight," Angel said. "Why don't you hold off until I've had a chance to talk to him? Maybe I can convince him that the whole thing needs a deeper look. The police are more likely to get involved if he backs you up."

"You're going to mention my thoughts about Damon and tell him about the property?"

Angel cleared her throat. Not exactly. Everett had already known about Damon, and Angel was sure he would agree with her that there was nothing much there when it came to Chloe's death. Damon and Chloe had likely had a brief fling, then went their separate ways after Everett had fired him. But Angel felt this new information about the property in Mexico might get his attention. "He needs to know everything if we want to try and convince him to get the police involved."

Paulette nodded slowly in agreement. "Makes sense. Okay. I'll wait to hear from you."

Angel sat back, relieved. The property purchase bolstered her view that Chloe had not taken her own life. She was happy, eager to start anew someplace else. Angel was now more convinced than ever that Ida must have had a hand in Chloe's end.

Love and jealousy made people do crazy things.

19

Angel couldn't stop pacing; back and forth she moved across the bedroom floor in her bare feet, her silk nightgown fluttering in the breeze.

She lifted her forearm, checked her wristwatch for the umpteenth time. Nearly ten thirty. Of course her husband would pick tonight of all nights to return home from work later than usual. She was exhausted, wanted nothing more than to dive into bed. But she would not get a wink of sleep even if she tried. Her world had been tossed upside down since overhearing the hushed conversation between Everett and his sister that morning. She had so much to share with him, so much to ask him. It felt like her head would burst.

Suddenly, she heard the double doors creak open. Her heartbeat quickened as she whirled around to face him. They still slept in separate rooms, but he always checked in on her before retiring if he'd missed her at dinner. The minute he laid eyes on her that evening, the smile disappeared from his face.

"What is it?" he asked. "You seem worried."

She opened her mouth to speak but her voice stuck in her

throat. She was so anxious to let it all out but also, scared. Here she was about to accuse his beloved sister of killing his first wife. Where and how should she begin? With the strange conversation she'd listened to that morning? With her raid on Chloe's room? The visit with Chloe's mom?

"Come, sit," she said softly, gesturing toward the sitting area. She had already tucked the love letters and airline ticket under a small antique African statuette on a table in the corner of the room.

"Well, damn," he said, following close behind her. "This seems serious." She sat on the couch; he walked to the minibar. "Okay if I pour myself a drink first?"

"Yes, please do."

"Can I fix something for you?" he asked, lifting a bottle of red wine.

She shook her head. Better not, she thought. She'd already downed two glasses, one with dinner, the other during her endless wait for him. She needed to keep her head clear for whatever lay ahead.

He poured himself a tall glass, sat next to her. "So. What's going on, sweetie? Why the . . . ?"

"I overheard the conversation this morning between you and Ida."

His eyes zeroed in on her, but she couldn't read them. Was he annoyed? Puzzled?

He sat up on the edge of his seat; his gaze trailed off to the side. "What exactly did you hear?"

"You and Ida seem really worried about me going into Chloe's room. I can maybe understand Ida. She's so possessive of Chloe and everything about her. But not you. She's your late wife. I'm your wife *now*. Why do you have such a big problem with it? And why did she ask what you had told me about that night?"

He drained his glass, stood up. She watched him patiently, silently, anxiously as he poured another drink.

"Well?" she blurted out as soon as he sat. "You would think you have something to hide."

He shook his head. "Not at all. I have no idea what's even in that room. I've only been in there once or twice since she died."

"Then why did you tell Ida someone should go through her things before I find them?"

He cleared his throat. "Chloe had a lot going on in her life. Not all of it was aboveboard, as you know. And she could be very secretive."

He was certainly right about that.

"We already talked about some of her . . . escapades," he continued. "I'll be the first to admit I was probably kept in the dark about a lot more. I'm sure there were things going on that I'm still unaware of. Just trying to protect her reputation. That's all."

She could accept that explanation, she supposed. "Well, I was in there this morning."

He stared at her, hard, his eyes full of doubt. "But it's always locked. How did you gain access?"

"Let's just say I found a way."

"Does Ida know about this?"

"I don't think so."

"Well, what? You picked the lock? Someone left it open?"

"What difference does it make how I got in? This is my house, too."

"Okay. So, what did you find? I'm assuming something is bothering you, something you want to tell me."

She hesitated. How did one go about revealing such devastating news?

She licked her lips, looked directly into his face. "I found love letters from Ida . . . to . . . to Chloe."

He shut his eyes, shook his head so slowly it was barely noticeable. He hopped up, undid his necktie. Now he was the one pacing up and down the floor. Angel figured he was having a difficult time processing what she'd just said.

She walked to the corner table, pulled the two letters from beneath the statuette, held them out to him. He recoiled, glancing at them as if she were offering him poison.

"Here. Read this."

He backed off. "I don't need to see that. I can't believe you're doing this."

Angel cocked her head to the side. Seemed like an odd reaction. Had Everett been suspicious of the relationship between Chloe and Ida all along? Or had he already known about it? No, that didn't make sense. The two would not be so close if that were the case. "Look, I hate to be the one to show you this. But you really should read them."

He reached out, snatched the letters from her grasp, and tore into one. His eyes quickly darted down the page, his expression growing more sour by the second. "Damn," he whispered, his face flushed with embarrassment.

"You also need to see this." She retrieved the airline ticket.

"What the hell?" he asked, grabbing it from her. "It's an airline ticket to Cabo San Lucas," he said after a cursory glance. "So what? I was not aware she planned to travel that week but I'm not surprised. She loved it there. She visited a lot, sometimes alone. Are you going to tell me she had a lover down there?" He scowled. "Wouldn't surprise me one bit."

"No, but if you read the other letter, you'll see that Chloe was planning to be away indefinitely, maybe permanently, and Ida was devastated about it. She begged Chloe to take her."

Angel could hear his breath quickening as he scanned the second letter.

"I really am sorry, Everett."

"Don't be sorry. What are you fucking sorry for? My late wife was a hot mess."

Yes, she was, Angel thought. But what about Ida? Chloe didn't have this affair behind his back all by herself.

"Have you mentioned any of this to Ida?" he asked. "About sneaking into the room and digging all this up?"

Angel chewed her bottom lip. She resented his characterization of her actions but didn't want to escalate the temperature now. He was already seething. "Of course not. I wanted to talk to you first."

"Well, now you have. I hope you understand you can never talk about any of this to anyone else. Ever. Can I count on that? I'll talk to Ida."

Angel frowned. That was it? This tepid reaction? She had expected him to be blown away by the news, upset, furious, even if he had been suspicious about the two of them. "There's more."

"More what?"

"I . . . I went to see Paulette."

He lifted his eyebrows. "Chloe's mom?"

"Yes."

"For Christ's sake, Angel. What the devil for?"

"She doesn't believe Chloe killed herself."

"Well, no. She'll never accept it. But why talk to *her*?"

"I wanted to understand her reasons for doubting it."

"That's obvious. She's a mother. What did you expect?"

"She also told me Chloe put a down payment on a house in Mexico the week before she died."

He blinked rapidly. "Seriously?" he said, sounding genuinely surprised. "I did not know about that."

"Do you see what this means?"

"So Chloe bought property. No big deal."

"Everett, no one buys property and then shoots themselves a week later."

Silence, as he seemed to ponder this. "Well, apparently she did."

Angel shook her head firmly. "No. I really doubt that."

"What are you trying to say, then?"

"Well . . ."

"The police ruled it a suicide. It's been settled."

"Maybe they made a mistake. They make mistakes all the time."

"Whoa. Angel, I don't like where I think you're going with this."

"Just hear me out, please, Everett. Ida was madly in love with Chloe."

He shook his head, licked his lips. "You need to stop this, Angel."

"You just read the letters. Ida begged Chloe to take her to Mexico. But based on what Paulette said, Chloe intended to go alone. At some point she would have told Ida no. And . . ." Angel hesitated. It was hard to get the next words out.

Everett squared his shoulders, as if bracing himself for what was coming.

"I . . . I don't know." Angel paused. Was she taking this too far? Was she being unreasonable, inconsiderate? No, no. She didn't think so. There were too many signs that this had not been a suicide, that something else had happened that night. "Maybe they argued and . . . and Ida shot her." There. She'd said it. Her true thoughts were finally out.

"I cannot believe I am hearing this. My wife just accused my sister of murdering my late wife."

"I mean, it could have been an accident. But don't you think . . ."

"Have you lost your fucking mind?"

She jumped back, startled. He had nearly spat the words in her face. Spittle lodged in the corners of his lips. He raised his hand, jammed a forefinger in her face. She took a step back and then another as he kept coming. "You are dead wrong, Angel," he said, his mouth twisted with bitterness. His voice bristled with anger. "My sister did not shoot my wife. How dare you."

He balled up the letters and ticket in his fists, threw them onto the couch. He gave her a final menacing glare and stormed out of the sitting room.

She exhaled, placed a hand over her heart. This was not going at all as she'd envisioned. Yet she could not leave it like this. She followed close behind, grabbed his elbow. "Everett, at least . . ."

He yanked his arm away. When he turned to face her, she noticed his bottom lip trembling. "Dammit. Will you stop this? You have no idea what you're saying."

"Look, Ev, I know it's hard to think about Ida doing something so awful but . . ."

"It's not hard, because I know she had nothing to do with it."

"How can you be so sure?"

"Because I was there, Angel." He pointed his forefinger at his own chest. "*I* shot Chloe."

❉   ❉   ❉

The room started spinning. She squeezed her eyes tight, opened them wide, shook her head to rid her mind of his words.

I shot Chloe.

"You don't mean that. You're just saying that to cover for her."

He sank down onto the cushioned bench at the foot of the bed and sat quietly for a moment. When he finally spoke, his tone was slow, soft, steady. "Unfortunately, it's true."

It felt like her brain was about to explode. "No, Everett. That can't be right."

"That night I made the biggest mistake of my life. It had been a tough year for the firm, and I worked a lot of late nights. That week there was a huge drop in the stock market. I spent days dealing with some very upset clients and their sinking investments. By Friday, I was bone-tired. I decided to come home a little early and . . ." He paused, swallowed. "I walked in on them. My cheating wife was in bed with my sister. Not with another man. Not with another woman. *With my sister.*"

So he had known about them, all along. Angel was shocked. She swallowed hard, looked him up and down from across the room, necktie loosened, shoulders drooping. Strangely though, she thought he looked relieved, like a huge weight had been lifted.

"In *my* bedroom, in *my* bed. Both naked." His voice was oddly serene now, almost a monotone.

"Oh, God," Angel whispered, trying to keep the visions out of her head.

"I'll spare you the details. But I had been thinking something was off with the two of them for months. They were always together. Planning menus, redecorating, shopping, laughing and joking. Never in my wildest dreams did I imagine they were lovers. This was a new low, even for Chloe. She had seduced my sister; it was too damn much. And I lost it. I fucking lost it." He lowered his head with sadness.

"Was Ida there when you . . . when it happened?"

"No. As soon as I walked in on them, she jumped up and ran down to her cottage. Chloe and I got into the biggest, nastiest argument. I told her I was sick and tired of her sleeping around. That it was over. She told me if I ever divorced her, she would take every dime I had. She threw things at me—a book, a mirror. She even had the nerve to brag about her affairs, her conquests. Said there were dozens but that she was entitled since I was never around and couldn't satisfy her."

He paused, buried his head in his hands. His shoulders shook, and Angel realized he was crying. A part of her wanted to go to him, to put her arms around him and console him. But she couldn't bring herself to do it. Not after what she'd just learned.

Finally, he lifted his head. "I could not get it out of my mind, her lying there with Ida. Chloe could be a cruel, twisted woman. So, I went into my closet. She stood outside the door screaming at me, yelling and calling me every name she could think of. *Bastard, asshole, wimp.* I grabbed the gun off the top shelf. I was going to try and scare her, to get her to shut her stupid mouth. But I . . . I shot her. As soon as I walked back out, the gun went off. A single bullet hit her in the chest. I knew immediately I had messed up."

Angel covered her mouth with her hand.

"Horrible, right?"

She ignored the question. The answer was obvious. "How did you convince the authorities it was suicide?"

"Ida planned that. She came running back when she heard the gun go off. The staff did, too, but we managed to keep them out of the bedroom. Ida was devastated. I had to smack her to get her to stop shrieking. Once she calmed down, though, she took the lead. Said she understood what I must have been going through. She blamed herself partly. When the police arrived, she told them that I was with her in the cottage when the gun went off. And that we found her together."

"Was there an investigation?"

"In the beginning, yes, but I was able to take care of that. A few bucks here and there in the right palms."

Angel didn't need to ask what that meant. So, Ida was in on the cover-up. Here she was blaming Ida and it had been Everett all along. If anything, Ida had saved her brother. This explained why he was always so deferential toward her. He owed her. It also explained why they both had so much to hide. The locked doors, the whispered conversations.

"So now you know everything."

She nodded. Unfortunately, yes, she did. But it was nothing like what she'd assumed. How wrong she had been. About Ida. About him. About that night. Shivers crawled up her arms.

"If you're going to turn anyone in, Angel, it should be me," he said. "Not her."

Angel knew he was expecting a response, but she had none. She was dumbfounded, numb. She walked slowly back into the sitting room and stood in front of the window, staring out at the black sky. She needed time to think. Here she had been ready to turn Ida in and her husband was the guilty one. Unbelievable. Unimaginable. Angel almost wished she could rewind the clock to before she'd gone snooping in Chloe's room. Given a second chance, she would mind her own business.

She went to her closet, threw a jacket over her nightgown, slipped into her running shoes. Then she brushed past him, still sitting there on the bench. She could feel his eyes following her every move.

"Angel," he said, jumping up as she approached the door. "Where are you going at this hour? It's almost midnight."

"For a walk," she said, her back toward him. She couldn't bear to look at his face. "I need some air."

Out the corner of her eye she saw him shove his hands into his pockets. "Before you talk to . . . to anyone, we should . . ."

"I'm not planning to talk to anyone tonight. I just need some time alone."

She strode out of the room, up the hallway, down the stairs. What she needed at that moment was to get far away from him, far away from this house.

She soon found herself running, stumbling across the dark, damp lawn, past the pool, past the gardens, with only the moonlight to guide her. Still, she didn't stop, feeling her way instinctively across the grounds of Riverwild that she had become so intimately familiar with. Eventually, she reached her favorite hilltop overlooking the river. This was her first time being out there so late at night. She couldn't see much of the river down below but she could hear the waters stirring, much like her heart.

She lifted her face to the twinkling stars and took in a generous breath of the fresh night air. Right now, it was hard to comprehend it all, impossible to get a grip on her feelings. Chloe had treated Everett shabbily. She'd had no idea how vicious and nasty the woman could be. Still, she had not deserved to die. And Everett should pay for what he'd done.

But could she turn in her own husband? Angel's stomach churned just thinking about what that would mean. They would probably throw the book at him. Yes, he was a billionaire and wealthy people often got away with things others couldn't. Yes, he had acted in a moment of provoked passion, and sentences for such crimes were sometimes less harsh. But Everett had a Black face, and all his wealth and passion might not matter in the end. He could be sent away for decades, maybe even for good. Their marriage would crumble. Her life would change drastically. Even if she were able to retain a sizable alimony, it would never feel the same without the man she had fallen in love with. The man who had brought her so much.

She buried her face in her hands. She knew what she *should* do. But *could* she?

20

She parted the bedroom drapes and squinted against the blazing morning sun. Then she closed her eyes and tilted her head upward to allow the warm glow to soothe her face. Just what she needed given the strange, monumental changes in her life over the past couple of months.

Angel peered over the expansive green lawn stretched before her, now dotted with the vibrant blossoming reds and brilliant yellows of late spring. Normally, she'd still be in bed at 7:20, and in another ten minutes, Janetta would enter to awaken her, ask if she wanted her coffee brought up. But Angel needed to begin this particular day with a moment to herself to reflect. It had been so long coming, there were times when she thought the day would never arrive. That events and people would forever push back, preventing any real joy in her life.

But the morning of their much-anticipated postwedding celebration was here. Finally.

Her husband walked up from behind, wrapped her in his arms.

"You okay?" Everett asked.

She rested her head on his shoulder. "Never better."

"Same here. I can't believe how well I'm sleeping lately. Feels like I owe you."

"Whatever for?"

"Allowing all this. *Allowing us.*"

"Wouldn't have it any other way."

He kissed her on the cheek. "Going to hop in the shower, then go out to pick up something special before tonight. Anything I can do for you before I leave?"

"Can you call the florist? We have two thousand sterling roses coming, and I want to be sure they're set up around the house on time." Sterling roses—lavender with silver undertones, a symbol of love and enchantment—were the perfect decoration for their momentous event.

"I thought I was paying an event planner and her team to handle those things?"

"You are, love, but she doesn't arrive until nine and I want to be sure this gets taken care of."

"Consider it done, sweetie," he said, walking off toward his dressing room.

She could stand at the window and marvel at the wonders of Riverwild Estate for hours; she had come to love the place that much. But that was not possible now. In little more than an hour, florists, caterers, bartenders, decorators, waiters, and the band would start arriving and darting around the main level of the mansion, and on the lawn, to set everything up for the festivities. All being guided by Olivia, the chef, and a well-known celebrity event planner. More than three hundred guests, including the Harrisons and Angel's friends Dawn and Patrice, were expected that evening.

Angel was supposed to stay on the third level with her dress designer and personal hairdresser as they put the final touches to her look, but she knew she'd never be able to do that with all the excitement buzzing in the air. She couldn't wait to stroll around, to have a look as things were being prepared. All the women would wear white for the black-tie event, except for her. Her couture gown was violet.

Janetta entered carrying a hot cup of coffee. "I figured you would want this for sure this morning."

Angel turned away from the window. "Yum," she said, taking a generous sip. "Just what I needed."

"Anything else I can do for you this morning, ma'am?"

Angel issued a few requests and Janetta ran off to draw the bath water. Slipping into the soaking tub a few minutes later, Angel thought about how for the first time since driving through the gates at Riverwild, she actually felt safe, secure, and in charge of her life. That might seem odd, considering she'd recently learned that her husband had shot and killed his first wife. The shocking revelation had exhausted her with worry for weeks. She had tossed and turned in the frenzy of nightmares too many nights to count. She'd climbed to her favorite spot on the hillside at Riverwild so often it was a wonder she hadn't beaten a dirt path through the lawn.

But the more she thought and the more she and Everett talked, the more her concerns eased away. She came to believe that Chloe had brought a lot of the animosity and bitterness to the marriage by treating Everett so badly. She questioned whether Chloe had ever really loved her husband or had only married him for his billions. It certainly seemed that she hadn't cared at all for him at the end. You couldn't treat a man like Everett, proud, dignified, refined, adored by so many, like dirt, day after day. That was the last thing he needed to come home to after a hard day's work. Angel now realized that although Everett was a tough and brilliant businessman, he was not invincible when it came to matters of the heart. Chloe must have sensed that, too, then used it to crush him when her own needs went unmet.

Angel knew better. The best approach with Everett was exactly the opposite—to love and support him in every way.

She had driven a hard bargain though. She admitted to him that she'd likely never have the heart to turn him in, but if he wanted her to stay and be the wife he needed, if their marriage were to work, there could be no more repeating the same patterns.

First, she insisted on no more guns in the house, period. Not now, not ever. And no more working late every night or sleeping in separate bedrooms. Next, Ida had to change or go. And by change, Angel insisted she must give up her place as manager of Riverwild and put Jackson in charge. Ida could continue to live there but would need to move into one of the spare bedrooms in the mansion and act as a sister and sister-in-law. Angel was done playing second fiddle to her. She was to be treated as the mistress of Riverwild or Ida was out. Everett had instantly agreed to all of these requests.

He had also, at her suggestion, purchased the property in Cabo San Lucas for Paulette by making an offer that the new owners couldn't refuse, paying them double what they had paid Paulette. It was not only a kind gesture to a bereaved mother who had lost her only child, unknowingly at his hand, but it also helped persuade Paulette to drop the nonsense about Damon and Chloe.

Best of all, she convinced him to purchase a waterfront property on Martha's Vineyard that she'd been eyeing for months. As she told Everett, she would love nothing more than to own a house on the island so she could return in style, and he wasted no time securing the $10 million estate. This was the moment Angel realized just how much he loved her and wanted her with him. They planned to leave for an extended stay the following week.

She could not have felt more content as she donned her violet gown that evening, admiring herself in the floor-length mirror in her dressing room.

"You look stunning," the designer said, zipping up the back. "This gorgeous color was made for you."

"She's a vision," her hairdresser added as she weaved a wreath of dried lilac flowers and crystals through Angel's natural hair. "This will top it off."

All three of them turned to see a tuxedoed Everett holding a square velvet jewelry box. He brought it directly in front of his wife and popped the lid to reveal a gleaming necklace of pink sapphires, rubies, and diamonds. They all gasped as he carefully draped the extravagant piece around her neck. Angel didn't mention that the gift had been a recent request from her as she turned and planted a big thank-you kiss on Everett's lips.

At the end of the evening, following the dancing and drinking and merriment, she exited the mansion on the arm of her husband, joining their illustrious guests for the planned fireworks display. As the two of them stood on the expansive balcony and looked up into the night sky, Angel realized that, finally, she truly felt like Mrs. Everett Bruce. Like Angel Bruce.

Angel.

Acknowledgments

This publication, my eighth novel and eleventh book, was yet another thrilling writing adventure. It was immersive and challenging, yet very gratifying in the end. I'm extremely grateful to those who helped me navigate along the way. First, Victoria Sanders, whose wisdom, experience, and tenacity are everything a writer could ask for in an agent. She has guided and supported me each step of the way from the very beginning more than thirty years ago. Next, my visionary editor Patrik Henry Bass at Amistad, who sees promise in this new direction for me as a writer, and his enthusiastic and helpful assistant, Francesca Walker. Then there's editor Benee Knauer, who is full of helpful insight and is a pleasure to work with.

Finally, as always, I'm thankful for my loving family and friends and their unwavering faith in me throughout the years.

About the Author

Connie Briscoe has been an author for three decades. Her novels have hit the bestseller lists of the *New York Times, Chicago Tribune, Washington Post, Boston Globe, Boston Herald, USA Today,* and *Publishers Weekly.* She has been featured in numerous publications and on television programs, including *Good Morning America.* She was born with a mild hearing loss that progressed over the years but has never let that stop her from pursuing her writing dreams. In 2003 she had a cochlear implant that restored much of her hearing. She lives in Maryland.